A VIRGIN TO REDEEM THE BILLIONAIRE

A VIRGIN TO REDEEM THE BILLIONAIRE

DANI COLLINS

MILLS & BOON

First published in Great Britain 2019
by Mills & Boon, an imprint of HarperCollins*Publishers*
1 London Bridge Street, London, SE1 9GF

Large Print edition 2019

© 2019 Dani Collins

ISBN: 978-0-263-08254-8

This book is produced from independently certified
FSC™ paper to ensure responsible forest management. For
more information visit www.harpercollins.co.uk/green.

Printed and bound in Great Britain
by CPI Group (UK) Ltd, Croydon, CR0 4YY

To my daughter Delainey, who was enlisted over Christmas to brainstorm an idea for a duet. "What comes in twos? How about something with earrings?" she suggested. *Voilà!*

Honorary mentions also go to my husband Doug, our son Sam, and Delainey's boyfriend Alex, who were all sounding boards as I regularly asked, "What if…?"

PROLOGUE

"LADIES AND GENTLEMEN, we've had a surprise offer for the entire estate by Mr. Kaine Michaels. A figure has been accepted by the family for the house and all the contents. We will not be auctioning individual items. Thank you for coming, but no further bidding will take place."

"What? *No.*" Gisella Drummond barely heard her own gasped words over the babble of discontent that rose from the crowd seated around her. They all let their bidding paddles droop in shock.

She instinctively looked to the tall stranger who had appeared in the room moments ago. He had captivated her as he entered to confer with the officials on a small dais near the fireplace. He was sinfully sexy in a suede jacket worn with casual elegance over black jeans and a button shirt without a tie.

Her first impression had been that his renegade appearance didn't fit this setting at all. The Manhattan mansion was a gorgeous ode to French Renaissance style, full of antique furniture placed with care on fading silk rugs under crystal chandeliers. Marble columns held up the low ceilings, and heavy velvet drapes blocked out the view of Central Park. That man was too rough around the edges for such a pristine, refined space. Had he really *bought* it, lock, stock and barrel?

Beside her, Mr. Walters cursed the man. He was one of her uncle's longtime business associates, had asked after her family and had confided he intended to buy the house.

Gisella was here only for an earring, but she was equally disappointed by this turn of events, probably more so. "Do you know him?"

"He owns Riesgo Ventures." Mr. Walters spoke with a disparaging sneer. "It's a tech company out of San Francisco. If he thinks he's earning any goodwill in this city with a move like that…"

She was curious what else Mr. Walters knew about him, but through the confusion of people rising and talking, she saw Kaine Michaels was leaving.

Urgency gripped her. She quickly excused herself and jostled as politely as she could through the milling bodies toward the door.

For a second, she thought she'd missed catching him. He wasn't exiting through the front doors of the entry foyer, though. His long legs had carried him up the wide, carpeted stairs to the gallery. He was moving along it with an auction house official hurrying to keep up.

She trotted up after him and pursued them down the hall. They paused at a pair of open double doors. The official spoke to the security guard standing watch.

"This is Mr. Michaels. He has just purchased the house and all of its contents. You can allow him to take anything he likes."

"Just the one piece," he said, indicating

something on the clipboard in the official's hand. "The rest can go into storage."

"Mr. Michaels," she called, wanting *one piece* herself before everything was sent to a remote, humidity-controlled facility.

He glanced back at her, then drawled to the guard, "Actually, you can go downstairs and show everyone the door."

The guard gave her a hard look, as if he meant to include her in his sweep.

She held up a hand. "I only need a moment."

Kaine jerked his head to dismiss the guard, then glanced at the official. The other man nodded and moved quickly into what looked like a sitting room. The jumble of paintings and sculptures wore numbered tags. So did a handful of furniture and other items. This was clearly the staging area for the auction.

The earring was probably among that collection, practically within reach. Butterflies of excitement batted around her midsection.

"Your moment is almost up," Kaine said.

She looked to him and lost her voice as she confronted his handsomeness up close.

His dark hair was short and thick, his brows bold statements above golden-brown eyes. His swarthy cheeks were smooth, but underlined by a precise border of stubble along his jaw. A goatee framed a mouth too full-lipped and sensual for words.

Men didn't usually affect her. Not even very good-looking ones, but a funny squiggle in her midsection teased with intrigue, especially when his eyelids lowered in lazy, male appreciation.

She extended her hand. "Gisella Drummond."

His relaxed demeanor altered. His expression tightened with dismay and he raked her with a more disparaging glance. It went down to her open-toed heels and came back to her snug top with the shoulder cutouts.

When he met her eyes again, she felt the impact as though she had walked into an invisible wall, one that teemed with icy electrical currents. They wrapped around her and squeezed the breath from her lungs.

He snorted in a way that suggested he couldn't believe her gall.

It was highly disconcerting. She was usually *very* well received by men. Not just for her various wealthy and respectable contacts, either. She was naturally blessed with the slender height and patrician bone structure seen in ads for swimsuits and makeup.

Her beauty was as much hindrance as strength so she didn't often use her looks for leverage, but this was battle conditions. She was on the verge of losing something she'd waited years to acquire.

She tried to melt his sudden frost with a warm smile, but it felt forced.

"I know who you are, Ms. Barsi." He only looked at her hand, didn't take it.

She let it drop along with her smile. Her heart also seemed to slump uselessly for a moment before she gathered herself with affront.

"I wasn't trying to misrepresent myself. I use my father's name." Not that it should matter either way. Her family was complicated, but she was a Barsi in her heart, if not by blood. The Barsis were a well-regarded family here in New York. Counting herself among them was an honor.

Yet it held no sway over him. If anything, her being one of them seemed to provoke a disdainful tic in his cheek.

"Sir?" the official said, returning from the auction room. "You're sure this is all you want for the moment?" He held a velvet box in his hands.

"Yes." Kaine moved into a nearby bedroom. His lip curled with distaste as he took in the canopied bed, the sitting area of ornate boudoir furniture and the heavy blue drapes framing a view over Central Park.

Gisella followed, wishing she'd been able to leave work early enough for the guided tour. It was a one-of-a-kind home and prime real estate. Her parents had money, but no one in Gisella's family was in a position to buy a house like this, especially if they didn't love it, which Kaine clearly didn't.

The official handed him the velvet box.

"I'll have the paperwork ready for you to sign when you come downstairs. Will you consider private offers on anything?"

"Everything but this. You can handle that for me?"

"Of course, sir." The official waited for Kaine's nod of dismissal, then hurried out, leaving Gisella alone with him.

Wait. He hadn't bought a house to get one item, had he?

Kaine tucked the velvet box into the pocket of his jacket without opening it.

Gisella's stomach swooped with dread. "What was that?"

She moved with panic to where a makeup table and dresser top held a number of open jewelry boxes, all with numbered tags on them. She scanned for the earring she'd only ever seen in the catalog for this auction. Several pairs of earrings were on display, but no orphans.

It wasn't here. She scanned again, her sense of loss visceral. She was going cold with shock while a shot of adrenaline hit her heart, sending a stinging throb through her limbs. How could she be this close after so long and *lose*?

"Was that an earring?" She swung around.

He gave her a blithe smile. *I know who you are, Ms. Barsi.*

She was fully taken aback. A wild suspicion came into her head and out her mouth before she'd had time to absorb how ridiculous it was. "You did not just buy a house to get that earring!"

"It was the most expedient means of getting what I want before anyone else."

Shock hit in waves. He really had bought the house for the earring. And there were other people after her grandmother's earring? Enough that he'd gone after it this aggressively? That made no sense. It was *one* earring.

"I don't know what you've been told, but it's not that valuable. It's not worth a *house*. Not *this* house. Why didn't you just bid on it?"

"Buying the house serves other purposes. And I don't have time to play game shows all day. Shall we?" He waved to invite her to leave.

"No." She put out a hand, used to having control of most situations, but she was utterly at a loss. It was the stakes, she told herself. She had been hunting that earring for more than a decade. She had been so sure she would take it home today and now her stomach was knotting with gross disappointment.

No. She straightened her spine, mentally smoothing the wrinkles from her normally smooth, aloof confidence.

"I'd like to make you an offer for it." He'd said he would take some, right?

On everything but this.

His expression grew both alert and satisfied. He cocked his head slightly, gaze scanning her features, taking his time studying her brow and cheekbones, her jaw and mouth. Almost as though he was memorizing them.

"Why do you want it so badly?" he asked. "If it's not that valuable?"

She licked her lips self-consciously while a scent of danger had her heart doing one of those skips that showed up in movies as a jag of returned life on heart monitors. Her whole body suffused with tingling heat. The air between them crackled.

"It has sentimental value for my grandmother." And her grandmother was growing frail. Gisella wanted to put it in her pale, elderly hand before another health issue arose to alarm all of them.

"You care about her very deeply." He seemed to delve into her soul with his piercing golden eyes.

"I do." A lilt of hope infused the words as she sensed he was coming around. "She's a very special woman."

"I'm sure you take after her." It was a thick piece of flattery, something she knew better than to fall for. Even so, his smoky voice caused her to blush.

It was inexplicable. He wasn't going out of his way to stoke the sexual awareness between them. She was simply aware it was there. Intensely aware. She didn't know why she was reacting to him so blatantly. She wasn't even sure she liked him. He seemed quite arrogant and ruthless.

But fascinating. She knew a lot of rich and powerful men. None radiated this innate confidence. None wore impervious armor that begged her to see if she could pierce it.

Maybe if she'd had lovers, she would have found her sensual side long ago, but she had a silly pact with her cousin to wait for that elusive thing Rozalia kept insisting was real— love.

Gisella had been humoring Rozi when she had made her vow of chastity. They'd been thirteen and sex had sounded ridiculous enough that Gisella had been happy to put it off. Until now, she hadn't met a man who had tempted her enough to break her promise.

But here she was, locking gazes in a staredown that filled her with anticipation. So much so, if he slid his attention downward, he'd see her nipples straining visibly against the lace of her bra and the light jersey of her top.

"How much would you like for it?" she asked, struggling to stay on task.

"It's not for sale."

He sounded so firm, so *smug*, she scowled in consternation.

"Such a beautiful face shouldn't wear such an angry frown." He ambled closer and grazed her jaw with the side of his knuckle. "It might stay that way. Shall we go?"

She ignored the way his light touch made her breath stutter and tightened her mouth with resolve. She was an only child, used to getting everything she wanted.

"How can I persuade you to change your mind?"

"You can't." His mouth pulled into a wicked grin. "But I'm tempted to let you try."

She narrowed her eyes. "I don't use sexual favors to get what I want," she informed him coldly. "If I kiss a man, it's because I want to." There. It was a dropped glove, but it was true. If she thought a man boorish, she told him so.

If she found a man enthralling… Well, he

was the first to fascinate her like this. She wondered if he might become her first in other ways. This power struggle was inordinately exciting.

"Is that so," he murmured. All the humor bled out of his expression, leaving it full of grave angles. He seemed to consider her words while the backs of his fingers continued to caress her throat where her pulse thrummed like a hummingbird's wings.

What was she doing? This was madness. He was a stranger. Voices were conversing in a nearby room.

But she wanted him to kiss her. It wasn't about the earring. He was unlike any man she had ever met. If he walked away and she didn't at least know what it felt like to have his mouth on hers, she would always wonder.

She stared into eyes that had become the incendiary gleam of liquid gold and dared him to make her day.

His hand came back to her jaw, his touch firm as he bent his head.

He claimed her mouth without ceremony,

as if they'd been kissing like this every night for years. And, oh, did he know how to kiss.

This was what she had sought all her life. A man who met her strong personality with an even stronger one. One who took her out of herself with a twist of his mouth against hers, parting her lips and sinking into a hungry, passionate ravaging that dismantled her even as he promised she would be safe in his strong arms.

She became a molten substance as he gathered her hair and squeezed an arm across her back. She pooled like quicksilver against him, curves fitting into the dips and contours of his chest, arms curling around his tense waist to settle her fingers against the warm hollow of his spine.

She had never been kissed like this. Carnal and possessive, urgent and lazy at once. Her scalp stung under the clench of his hand in her hair. Heat consumed her, burning up any memory she had of other men. A moan of pleasure escaped her, but it contained loss. She understood that every kiss that had come before this one had been a manufactured fraud. This was the real thing. She could never settle for less again.

And he was already pulling away.

Her lips clung to his as his hand moved to the side of her face. His mouth lifted away. It was too soon. A sob of protest arrived as a lump in her throat. His breath was as ragged as hers, feathering across her wet lips. She refused to open her eyes, not wanting him to see how completely he had owned her in this too-brief encounter.

He knew, though. He spoke in a gravelly whisper that caressed her cheek and lifted the hairs on her scalp. "I'll lock the doors and take everything you're offering, but you're not getting the earring."

"What?" She blinked her eyes open and the world came back into focus. She saw the colorful mural on the ceiling, the gilded light fixture. Its glow haloed his dark hair, turning him into an archangel.

"A valiant effort, though."

She made herself step back, feeling the loss

of his heat like a splash of icy water down her front. The barest hint of her lipstick shaded his mouth. She wanted to use her thumb to erase it. She wanted to keep touching him. Lock the doors and stay in here and discover everything he could teach her.

She had always wondered what it would feel like to discover her chemical match. To be devoured by true, animalistic passion.

It was terrifying, as it turned out. Deliriously perilous, yet treacherously alluring.

"That wasn't—" She cut herself off as she absorbed the jaded look in his eyes. Which was a harder kick to her pride? His thinking she had been trying to manipulate him? Or confessing her passion had been real when his was clearly nonexistent?

"Here comes the frown again. I didn't expect you'd take this so hard." The corners of his mouth deepened in a curl of merciless amusement. "It makes denying you what you want so much more satisfying."

Her ears rang with the double entendre

while her scrambled brain finally began to comprehend what was going on.

"Are you telling me you're doing this as some sort of vendetta against me?"

"What I'm doing—" his voice turned to granite "—is getting your cousin's attention." His tone was hard enough to make her insides shiver with foreboding. "Pass the message along. I expect a phone call."

CHAPTER ONE

One week later...

"DID YOU SEE my text? I asked you to pick up lattes." Gisella pouted with disappointment as her cousin, Rozalia, showed up empty-handed in their workroom above the family jewelry store, Barsi on Fifth.

"I didn't look at my phone." Rozi peeled off her raincoat and hung it, but missed the hook so the coat dropped to the floor with a *flump* and a spatter of raindrops. She didn't notice, only splaying out her hands as though stopping traffic. "I have big news."

Gisella bit back scolding her cousin. Their mothers were half şisters and a decade apart in age. Rozalia had been born a few months after Gisella, but they had had very different upbringings. Gisella's mother, a career academic, had had her one baby late in life. At the sight of a dropped jacket, she would have stridently pointed out the need to keep everything neatly in its place, especially when all Gisella's clothes were top-brand and tailored.

Rozalia's mom had married young and lived for her husband and four children. For her, *things* didn't matter. People did—which was why Gisella had always envied Rozi and secretly wished they were twins instead of cousins.

"Someone—" Rozi said with great drama, because her family was nothing if not rife with artists and performers "—wanted a deal on a custom engagement ring."

"That's nice," Gisella said mildly. Such things were their bread and butter, but she knew better than to insist Rozi get to the point. She was clearly eager to make a Broadway production out of this. "Who would that be?"

"An agent. For an auction house." Rozi touched her chin and lifted a musing gaze to the ceiling. "A firm that may or may not have handled the Garrison estate last week."

Gisella's heart dropped to roll around the legs of her work stool. It took everything in her to pretend she didn't go both hot and cold with yearning and embarrassment. Fury and shame.

She felt so foolish for letting Kaine kiss her. She had been lost in some deranged space between flirting and taunting when she invited it. She wouldn't have let him touch her, however, if she'd known he was exercising some kind of *wrath* against her family. His toying with her, kissing her the way he had, was just *wrong*.

I'm getting your cousin's attention.

His detachment had driven the spike of his rebuff that much deeper. It still stung like mad.

Gisella turned back to the empty platinum pendant setting pinched in the vise on the bench. "We know who won everything at that auction."

And who had *lost*.

She had. Even her dignity had been left in that room full of a dead woman's valuables as she'd rushed to get away from him.

"Oh, forget Kaine Michaels. Or rather, remember what he said about other interested parties? There was a representative on the phone, calling from Hungary."

Gisella set down her wheel and lifted her magnifying glasses as she swiveled to face Rozi again. "So?"

"He was calling on behalf of Viktor Rohan. According to the agent, he was—" she air quoted with her fingers "—highly motivated to buy the match to the one his mother possesses."

"Oh, my God, Rozi."

"I *know.*"

Sixty-odd years ago, the earrings had been sold months apart on different continents. Finding the one here in America had been years of hard work. They had long ago given up finding the other one, hitting nothing but dead ends every time they tried.

"Guess what else? He's your *cousin.*"

"Viktor Rohan? I've never even heard of him." She fully pulled off her eye protection and set it aside. *"How?"*

"Second cousin, I guess. Your grandparents were brother and sister."

"He's descended from Istvan's sister?"

Rozi nodded.

Istvan had asked their grandmother, Eszti, to marry him when they'd been at university together. He'd given her a pair of earrings as an engagement present and she should have married him and kept those earrings all her life. Instead, student demonstrations had turned violent. At Istvan's urging, Eszti had sold one of the earrings in Hungary to come to America, unwed and pregnant. Her lover had died before he could follow as promised, leaving her alone in a new country.

Broke and desperate, with Gisella's mother an infant in her arms, Eszti had married Benedek Barsi, a kind, older man. A goldsmith. Benedek sold the second earring and they started the jewelry store where both Gisella and Rozalia now worked. Eszti was grandmother to both of them, but Gisella didn't have any Barsi DNA. She had Istvan's blood—which was how she could be related to Viktor Rohan where Rozi wasn't.

"Have you never been curious about that side of your family?" Rozi asked her.

"Oh, please. You know what Mom is like. But I agreed with her lack of sentiment in this case. Grandpapa always treated us like we were his. I was never so curious I wanted to hurt him by looking into Grandmamma's first love. It wasn't like I could meet Istvan. He died before my mother was born." Gisella shrugged it off.

"But you're curious now?" Rozi pried, grinning.

"If he has the other earring, of course I am!"

They laughed and Rozi clapped her hands and bounced in her lace-up boots. "Think of what it would mean for Grandmamma, Gizi."

"Let's not get ahead of ourselves," Gisella cautioned. They had both dreamed for years of returning the earrings to their grandmother, but Gisella had just had her dream popped like a soap bubble by that wretched Kaine Michaels. Oh, she never wanted to think about him again! "Viktor lives in Hungary? What sort of person is he?"

"Rich! He has homes all over Europe, far as I can tell, but he has a family home in Budapest. His mother lives there. I have an email address for her. I'm thinking you should see if she's willing to meet you, seeing as you're a long-lost relative and all."

"Will do. What's your workload like? Can you get away for a bit?" For the first time in a week, the sun broke past the dark clouds inside her, sending warm beams of excitement through Gisella.

"I could, but—" Rozi gave a small wince.

"If it's money, don't even. You know I'll cover your side of it." Along with her comfortable income from her work here at the jewelry store, Gisella's parents were very well-off. Her mother was shrewd with investing and had no one to inherit her fortune except her one child. Gisella's father had set aside a generous trust that he regularly topped up with dividends from his advertising business.

Rozi had the same private education paid for by their grandparents as all the cousins had been afforded, but Rozi's parents had always lived paycheck to paycheck. Rozi supported herself and didn't have a buffer.

"I could make the finances work," Rozi said with a scowl of insult. "But I'm worried about the earring Kaine Michaels has. It sounds like Viktor has been making offers to him. I know you said it looks like a lost cause there. Tell me again what he said about Benny?"

"I *presume* he was talking about Benny," Gisella muttered.

At first, she'd been convinced Kaine had been referring to Rozi. Whenever anyone mentioned her cousin, Gisella's thoughts always went to the one who'd been her constant companion since they'd been infants. While Gisella's mother had worked, Rozi's mother had minded Gisella like one of her own. She had pushed Rozi and Gisella in a side-by-side stroller, braided their hair into matching pigtails, dressed them in each other's clothes and dropped them on the same day into the same kindergarten classroom.

Gisella had a half-dozen cousins, though. Along with Rozi's three siblings, their uncle Ben had two children. All of them were as dear to her as the next. Kaine could have been talking about any of them that day. However...

"Benny's the only one I haven't been able to reach," she said, hating herself for doing exactly as Kaine had asked. She had spoken to each of her cousins in turn, trying to pass along his message. "Everyone else has said they've never met him. When Uncle Ben gets back from Florida, I'll ask him where Benny is. See if there's a way to reach him. Even so—"

"I know. Benny can be a rascal, but he wouldn't hurt a flea."

"Exactly."

Yet Kaine Michaels had some kind of grudge against him. It didn't make sense.

"Well, I know you don't want to talk to

Kaine, but I think we should make another offer. If we're going to get these earrings, now is the time. Before…"

Gisella knew what Rozalia was hesitating to say aloud. Their grandmamma was eighty-one and recovering in Florida from a bad bout of pneumonia she had suffered this winter. It was a stark reminder they were running out of time to get the earrings back to a woman they both loved with all their hearts.

"I won't go to San Francisco, if that's what you're suggesting." Gisella never wanted to see Kaine Michaels again in her life. "He hates me." The contempt was mutual.

"No, you should go to Hungary," Rozi agreed. "The Rohans are your relatives. I'll take a crack at Kaine Michaels myself."

Something in Gisella screeched and fish-tailed. Rozi was pretty in a wholesome way with thick brunette hair, a creamy complex-ion and a trim if almost boyish figure. She didn't draw men as inexorably as Gisella's more classic and voluptuous attributes. They had never been rivals for a man and Gisella didn't want Kaine anyway!

Even so, she felt oddly threatened by her cousin approaching him. If anything, she ought to be worried he would crush tender Rozi even worse than he'd managed to dent Gisella's more stalwart soul. They had exchanged a few words and one kiss. He shouldn't have left her feeling so trampled and discarded. She was stronger than that.

Maybe Rozi's earnest and engaging personality would inspire a kinder response in him. Persuade where she had failed. She ought to let Rozi at least try. For Grandmamma.

"I always thought if I went to Hungary, we'd go together," Gisella said sullenly.

"Me, too." Rozi made a face. "I'm dying to learn more about the earrings. And look at this guy." Rozi pulled her phone from her pocket to show her a photo. "Tell me he's not reason enough for a ten-hour flight."

Gisella glanced at the photo under a headline claiming Viktor Rohan was Europe's most eligible bachelor. He was very handsome, but she noted his good looks the way she recognized that her other male cousins were attractive—objectively and without stirrings of feminine interest. He didn't produce a fraction of the heat in her blood that merely thinking about Kaine did.

"Have them both," Gisella said, determined to stop thinking about Kaine. "I'm swearing off men. They're a waste of my precious time."

Rozi chuckled and looked at the photo again, voice softening to a dreamy whisper. "What if we could actually get the earrings for Grandmamma, Gizi?"

"I would love that," she said with equal yearning.

The tale of the earrings had always struck a chord in her. It had been such a huge sacrifice on Grandmamma's part. Ezti had sold a cherished gift from her lover to buy a fresh start in the New World. That bold move had been the foundation for the abundant life Gisella enjoyed. How could she not be moved and thankful? How could she not want to repay her grandmother by getting back the earrings that should have been hers all this time?

"Let's do whatever it takes," Gisella said, growing solemn and holding out her pinkie.

They linked their little fingers the way they'd done a thousand times when making a pact. "For Grandmamma."

CHAPTER TWO

KAINE MICHAELS WASN'T surprised when
he saw Gisella Drummond enter the private
lounge where his staff was celebrating his
latest app going public. He was furious, of
course. She was deliberately misunderstanding him, but he had to admire her moxie.

You're not the cousin I want to talk to, he
had replied to someone named Rozalia when
she had tried to set up a meeting a few days
ago.

Gisella wasn't either, but he found he wasn't
disappointed. Maybe he'd even left his word-
ing open to interpretation, curious to see if
she'd make another attempt to "persuade"
him.

She really ought to be ashamed of herself,
walking in here without an invitation, but
he doubted she possessed such a thing. For

starters, where would she keep it? There was absolutely no room for anything but sex appeal in that little black dress she was almost wearing.

He had thought her stunning when all he'd seen of her was loose waves of caramel hair, a slender back and an ass that could stop traffic atop legs that went for miles.

Tonight, she captivated him just as easily and completely. How? This was California. Beautiful women were low-hanging fruit here. He didn't have a type, but found himself partial to everything about her. Her height, her buttermilk skin, her elegantly refined bone structure.

In a land where everything was fake from eyelashes to teeth to breasts, she stood out as a natural beauty. She wore makeup, but not a candy coating of it. Hers was applied in subtle shades that accentuated her high cheekbones and glossed her luscious mouth.

Coders in sweatshirts and khakis turned their heads to watch as she wove toward

Kaine. The twenty-somethings adjusted their glasses and the forty-somethings sucked in their stomachs. The women in pencil skirts narrowed their eyes with envy.

Her aloof expression took no notice of anyone except him as she moved through mirror-ball sparkles that glittered off glowing white twigs against a bath of purple light cast by black bulbs.

"Gentlemen," she said as she arrived into his circle. She barely raised her voice above the thump of the DJ's playlist, neatly interrupting a movie producer trying to talk Kaine into investing in his latest blockbuster. "I need Mr. Michaels."

Kaine had an idea where her audacity came from. Her father owned a well-respected advertising firm. She'd been raised in upper-class circles thanks to a private education. Even so, she was a goldfish, not a shark. One who still managed to blow a few bubbles and shoo the bigger fish away. They dispersed without hesitation, only looking over their shoulders to catch a glimpse of her slinky black dress and slinkier shoes.

Those tiny black patent belts enclosing her ankles would inspire a fetish in a priest.

Kaine dragged his attention back up her legs, fantasizing about the smoothness of those thighs against his palms and lips. Was she wearing matching midnight underwear beneath that short skirt? A wink of red? Something nude? Perhaps she *was* nude.

He bit back a groan of craving, dying to find out. And the top of that thing. He could ease it down with a fingertip and discover exactly how warm and round and heavy her perfectly formed breasts were. Lick at her nipples and watch a flush of pleasure stain her skin.

He arrived at cheeks hollow with dismay. Her eyes—green, he recalled, since the surreal lighting made the color indiscernible—shot sparks of indignation.

"You crashed this party, Ms. Barsi," he pointed out, refusing to apologize for his ogling. "Don't complain about the reception you receive." He added a laconic, "Call security," to the waiter who approached with a tray of champagne.

The server faltered.

"He's joking," Gisella said, stealing a flute of bubbly and smiling in a way that dazzled the confused server into smiling and ducking his head.

"I'm not," Kaine assured her as the kid slipped away.

She only sipped and glanced over the crowd. "You call this a party?"

A deserved burn. The atmosphere was flatter than roadkill. Despite the pulse of music and the money made by everyone in the room, people stood in knots of downcast heads. Kids these days. They'd rather post a photo that they were there than *be* here.

"It's Drummond, by the way. I told you that last week," Gisella said. "When my grandmother married Benedek Barsi, she already had my mother."

"Did she?" He scratched under his chin.

She sent him a sharp look. "What does that mean?"

"I do my homework." Did she really not know?

He'd been intrigued by her from the first photo he'd seen, gaze drawn back to her image more than once as he'd learned all he could about Benny's family. A few things had converged to make buying the Garrison estate a wise, last-minute move. He might not have been there, however, if his attention hadn't already been snagged by her. His sources had revealed she'd been searching for a single earring for years and he'd seen an opportunity.

And, if he hadn't known about her intense interest, he might have believed she'd been responding to his kiss in a very open, refreshing way. She hadn't, of course. She had been trying to manipulate him. Even knowing that, he remained reluctantly fascinated.

"Have you been doing yours?" he asked her.

"My homework?"

"Yes. How is Benny? Never mind. I don't care. Unless he's dead. That's the only excuse I'll accept for his avoiding my calls."

Pressing her lips flat, she seemed to gather her composure, standing taller and squaring her shoulders. "I haven't been able to reach him."

"Then why are you here?"

"You know why. The earring. You wouldn't meet Rozi so here *I* am. I'm willing to be generous."

"Not interested," he lied. He was far too interested in watching how she played this despite knowing she was trying to play *him*.

"I haven't even given you a number."

He shrugged. "Whatever you offer, I can receive double from someone else."

"Viktor Rohan?"

For some reason, the way she said the man's name—pithy and familiar—provoked a sudden, inexplicable tension in him.

"You know him?" He kept his poker face

on, pretending equal disinterest as he scanned the crowd.

"I know *of* him. We haven't met. You're planning to sell it to him, then?" She was affecting nonchalance, same as him, but she had tells. Her fingers tapped the stem of the glass she held, betraying her nervous interest in his answer.

"I haven't decided."

Viktor Rohan had become a bit of a thorn in Kaine's side, prodding him to sell the earring to him with ever-increasing incentives. Kaine wasn't playing him like a fish. From what he knew about the man, Rohan wasn't a man to be trifled with. Under other circumstances, Kaine would have happily parted with the bauble for a modest profit.

But then, Gisella would have no reason to be here, frowning over his funeral of a party.

"What if I say I'll double Viktor's last offer?" she asked.

Kaine was again impressed by her bravado.

He named the most recent figure Viktor had sent him, which made her lashes quiver.

He smirked. "Ready to fold?"

"I'm not bluffing," she bluffed. "I just hadn't realized how quickly the stakes were rising. I'm prepared to pay that. Do we have a deal?" She offered her free hand.

"Oh, hell no. I don't need the money and it's clearly appreciating daily." The value of its leverage with *her* was priceless.

He sipped his bourbon and her arm fell to her side.

"You're quite desperate for this thing, aren't you? Why?" The earring was pretty, Kaine supposed, but he didn't see what all the fuss was about. "To sell it to Rohan yourself at a profit?"

"No." She acted offended. "I told you. I want to give it to my grandmother."

"One earring."

"It's very special to her."

Kaine had never understood attaching emotion to anything, least of all musty old objects. He didn't even possess a favorite pair of jeans let alone a watch or a boat that he would grieve over sinking. Everything could be replaced, provided he kept his bank balance healthy enough to make the purchase.

As someone gambling in the tech industry, he didn't even let the fluctuations in his cash flow bother him too greatly.

The only time he grew hot under the collar was when someone tried to take something from him. And someone had. A few weeks ago, her cousin Benny had blown a crater into Kaine's net worth. The circle of investors whom Benny had assembled were all standing around the edge, throwing rocks to ensure he sank as quickly as possible.

That was a memory to hang on to, not the one where he had clasped that pointed chin and ravaged those pillowy lips with a hunger that sat in the pit of his gut right now, howling like a starving beast scenting more.

"I can't be swayed by emotion," he informed her, trying to burn away his ferocious thirst for her by finishing his neat bourbon in one fiery swallow. He cut his gaze down her front with dismissal, determined she wouldn't know how thoroughly she was getting to him. "Not even by lust."

Gisella had dressed to get past security without a lot of questions. There were always a few mistresses and trophy wives at events like this. All she'd had to say was, "I'm meeting my husband," and she had sailed on in.

Now, however, as Kaine Michaels skimmed an appraising gaze over her while cynicism dug a curl into the corner of his mouth, she grew hot and wished she'd chosen a power suit.

At the same time, her brain picked apart his remark. Was he saying he felt lust toward her? That ought to offend her, not cause a seesaw of excitement and yearning. A flood of heat that was more pleasure than outrage began licking low in her belly.

She couldn't help being deeply attracted to him, though. He'd been a force in a shirt with an open throat and suede jacket. Tonight, he wore a tuxedo with satin lapels over a shirt with hidden buttons. He ought to look like every other man in here, but from the cut of the shoulders to the break in his pant cuff over shiny handcrafted Italian shoes, he was a man above the rest. One who knew it, too.

Trying to hide how deeply he mesmerized her, she said, "If I was here to seduce you, you would know it."

The white of his teeth flashed. It wasn't so much a smile of amusement as satisfaction. "I like a sense of humor, especially in my enemies. It keeps me from growing bored."

"How am I your enemy? You're angry with Benny." If she left with nothing else tonight, she would understand why he was taking out his anger on her. "Tell me what you think he did."

"I know what he did," he said, turning so cold it was as if a door had been thrown open to the Arctic. A subzero blizzard swirled around her with his words. "He falsified mining samples and disappeared, framing me to look like the culprit. I've made explanations to my investors, but they aren't buying it."

"Wait, what?" She found her hand on his arm of its own accord, needing to steady herself.

He was like iron under the fabric of his jacket sleeve. He looked at her hand with a raised brow, making her lift it away self-consciously. Her pulse continued to bounce like a pinball.

She fought to recover and find her voice. Benny was a geologist. His exploration company operated as an arm of Barsi on Fifth. It allowed Barsi on Fifth, her *employer*, to offer its richest clientele a means of investing in gems and precious metals literally at ground level.

"Benny would never salt samples. Our entire family relies on the Barsi reputation remaining impeccable. We all do our part to keep it that way."

"Yes, it would seem all of New York believes your family is beyond reproach. That's why the investment consortium is blaming *me* for the fraud, turning my name to mud all the way down the Eastern Seaboard."

She shook her head, wanting to sit down, but the room was nothing but high-top tables, glittering ice sculptures and gaggles of hoodies. The music and noise were getting to her and she noticed that people were watching them. It made her uncomfortable, now that Kaine had completely thrown her out of her element. She had to fight letting the cracks in her composure show.

"What exactly has Benny said?"

"*Nothing.* That's why I had to get his attention. You've disappointed me, Gisella. I don't think you want that earring nearly as badly as you pretend. I think you're more interested in keeping Benny's crime from coming to light. You're trying to placate me. But this sort of mollification—" he circled his finger to encompass her painted lips to her painted toes "—is very last century. And entirely too predictable."

His accusation sent a few more fractures zigzagging across her veneer of confidence. She had *wanted* to kiss him, not that she would admit it now. Not when he was so disparaging about something that had caused such a flagrant reaction in her it still put a scorch of vulnerability in her throat.

"Benny is probably at the site, trying to sort it out," she insisted.

"The site is in Indonesia. His office said he's in South America. So does his social media."

"I'll make some calls. Right now."

"Knock yourself out."

Her heart hammered like a trapped bird in her chest, unsure which direction to fly. With a sniff of determination, she moved into a quiet corner and quickly realized it was well past business hours in New York, even later in South America. She tried her uncle's cell, biting her nail because he might not even pick up. He was still in Florida checking on Grandmamma and they might be having an early night.

He answered and they exchanged brief greetings. He was her boss at Barsi on Fifth along with being her uncle. He presumed she was calling about work.

"No, it's about Benny," she said. "Have you

spoken to him lately? I've just heard the most bizarre rumor from Kaine Michaels." She glanced around, not wanting to repeat what Kaine had said in case she was overheard.

Her uncle's silence was very ominous.

"Uncle?" she prompted.

"Why are you talking to *him*?" She couldn't tell if his inflection was disdain or trepidation.

"Kaine has Grandmamma's earring. I tried to buy it at an estate auction last week." She hadn't told anyone what she was planning, wanting to surprise everyone with her triumph. Instead, things had spiraled into a bigger mess than she could have anticipated. "I came here to make him an offer, but he's making some awful accusations. Benny needs to call Kaine right away and straighten this out."

"For God's sake, Gisella. I wish you had talked to me first."

"Why? What's going on?" A chill invaded her chest.

"I don't know," he said in a clipped voice.

"I've heard the few rumors myself. I'm doing my best to quash them while I try to get hold of Benny and hear his side of it."

"You don't think he would actually—"

"I do *not*," he assured her, believing as she did that Benny was honest, reliable and professional. "But I don't trust Michaels. You shouldn't, either."

She glanced up and saw Kaine staring at her from across the room.

"He wouldn't be this angry if he didn't feel it was justified." She understood that instinctively.

"Well, don't antagonize him further," her uncle ordered. "He's a dangerous man."

In many ways. He held her from afar with nothing more than an unbroken stare.

"I'll, um, do my best to smooth things over. Explain that we'll have answers soon." A dent in the Barsi name could spell disaster for all of them.

"I'll try Benny right now," her uncle promised. "Tell Michaels I'll have him get in touch as soon as possible."

She doubted that would be enough for Kaine, but Gisella thanked him and ended the call. As she did, she noticed a message from Rozi. Her cousin had touched down safely in Hungary and was headed to her hotel for a nap.

Viktor Rohan's mother had agreed to meet with Gisella after Gisella had leaned heavily on their distant bloodline connection. Gisella had been completely prepared to go herself, but Kaine had rebuffed Rozi's request for a meeting with his annoying, *You're not the cousin I want to talk to.*

In a fit of pique, Gisella had insisted Rozi take her meeting with the Rohans. *She* would handle Kaine Michaels. This time he wouldn't get the better of her.

She had believed it right up until Kaine's accusation had left her bobbing through the ether, completely unmoored. Benny would not have committed fraud. That much she knew. It wasn't in his nature and he wouldn't put the family's reputation and livelihood in jeopardy.

"Can I get you a drink?"

Gisella glanced up to see a handsome thirty-something in a nice suit eyeing her as if she was the dessert selection of the buffet. He might have been one of the men talking to Kaine when she arrived, but she hadn't taken much notice of anyone but the man she'd come to see.

"Finished your call?" Kaine said, appearing at her side with ninja suddenness. "Darling," he added, dry and late with the endearment, clearly using it to step on the other man's advances.

The other man melted away.

Kaine lightly skimmed his hand to the small of her back, setting her senses alight, breaking her voice as she tried to answer his question.

"Y-yes. My uncle will have Benny call you as soon as possible."

"Wonderful," he said with open sarcasm. "Let's dance, then."

She didn't want to *antagonize him further*, but, "No one is dancing."

"Leaders lead. You strike me as one."

She snapped him a look, but that hadn't sounded like more sarcasm. It seemed to be a sincere compliment. How would he know what she was like?

"Why else would you be here representing your family?" he taunted lightly. "You're not a sacrificial lamb, are you?"

"No." But she felt inordinately vulnerable. She had been thinking of him day and night, trying to hate him even as she had wished things had gone differently. Wished their kiss had been the beginning of something more.

That longing was still lodged in her throat with a sob of disappointment. At least now she understood why he was treating her with such disparagement.

This had to be a misunderstanding. Had to be.

And she *was* an independent sort. One who struck out on her own to get things done. One who would happily play envoy for her family, even if she found it uncomfortable to face down so much suspicion.

"Why don't we take this discussion somewhere more private," she suggested.

His eyes became narrow slits with a gleam of enigmatic obsidian. His smile was empty of humor as he drew his lips back against his teeth.

"That would be my pleasure."

CHAPTER THREE

KAINE IGNORED THE disappointment that hit him as she more or less admitted to being here to keep him from taking stronger action against her family.

He shouldn't be letting her under his skin. Aside from retaliating when someone tried to knock him down, he never allowed anyone to affect him on an emotional level, let alone a woman attempting to toy with him.

This turnaround from her innocent act when she'd arrived told him that's exactly what this was: pure manipulation. Worse, when she had been protesting ignorance where her cousin's behavior was concerned, she had nearly caused him to doubt his own sound judgment. He had found himself thinking maybe she really did just want to buy an earring for her grandmother.

As she had stepped away to make her call, he had actually allowed himself to imagine her coming back to him with a rational explanation, one that would allow him to believe in her, fool that he was. He had learned long ago that trusting people, particularly a woman he physically desired, resulted only in an empty wallet.

He sure as hell hadn't intended to come to heel like a poodle on a leash, but another man had approached her. The possessiveness that had engulfed him in those seconds had been so intolerable, it propelled him across the room to stake a claim.

It was time to yank back control. He texted his driver as they exited the private rooms of the restaurant. When she veered toward the bar, he said, "We'll go to my place."

She faltered, then said, "I'm getting my bag. I haven't checked into my hotel yet."

Convenient. After she'd handed her ticket to the coat check, he picked up the small case and escorted her out. His car smoothly rolled to the curb and he opened the back door himself.

* * *

Kaine's driver dropped them in front of a mirrored skyscraper with a lobby that led onto a restaurant.

Gisella glimpsed more than one starlet standing in line, but Kaine didn't take her into that hot spot. He waved her into an elevator set back from the rest, one she quickly realized was his alone since his thumbprint made it whisk upward.

The darkened bay and the lights outlining the bridge came into view. Before she'd had a chance to process that, the windows went dark again. The elevator came to a stop, the doors opened and—

"Oh." Glass walls offered more than 180 degrees of night sky and ocean. The sparkle of city and moonlight on the water, bobbing boat lights and stars against an inky sky drew her into the penthouse. The open-plan rooms were lit by a subtle glow in the baseboards and a single table lamp. He didn't turn on any other lights.

A rational part of her warned this might be

dangerous, coming to a strange man's apartment. Things were contentious between them, but, "This is so *beautiful*."

She wanted to see it in daylight, eat breakfast on that veranda protected by glass that would let in the sun but keep out the wind. She wasn't a covetous person, but she rather wanted this.

He moved behind the wet bar and opened a bottle of wine. She felt his gaze on her across the football field that was his living room. The horseshoe sofa would seat twenty, the dining table equally as many. The kitchen seemed to be tucked around the far side of the dining area and she suspected the stairs over the bar led to his bedroom.

She glanced at the big screen. It looked as though it disappeared into the wall at the flick of a button. It didn't have game controllers attached, which surprised her. He made a large chunk of his fortune in that arena.

"Do you host a lot of parties?" The place was built for entertaining, but something in his persona told her he kept his space private.

He was such an infuriating man. She wanted to hate him for the accusations he kept throwing at her, but she was intrigued despite herself.

"You're one of a handful of people who have been here since I moved in two years ago. The maid and doorman are my most frequent guests. My PA sometimes."

"The inner sanctum," she murmured, moving forward to stroke the buttery leather of the sofa. "I'm flattered."

Was the earring here? She glanced around, wondering if it was in a safe behind that abstract painting in the dining room. He probably had an office upstairs.

"It's in a safe-deposit box at my bank," he said, reading her mind.

She crossed her arms, annoyed with herself for being so obvious.

"I brought you here for privacy. To discuss the terms of your compensation."

"You keep accusing me of being willing to barter sex for favors. You know that says more about you than me, right?" She refused to gauge the distance to the elevator, tingling at speaking so frankly, but not with danger. It was the excitement of dropping a layer of civility. Like peeling off her cloak and letting him see what she wore beneath.

"I don't pay for sex," he drawled, moving around the horseshoe of the sofa to bring her wine.

"No?" she scoffed gently, taking it and speaking into the aromas of honey and peach before flavors of oak and vanilla dampened her tongue. "You don't bring lovers on vacation? Buy them a parting gift of a bracelet or necklace?" She didn't take such commissions on purpose, but knew some of her pieces had been bought by older men who had given them to women who weren't their wives.

"Inviting someone to join me on my yacht is hardly paying for her company." He picked up a tendril of her hair and drew it across the front of her neck like a collar. "And my lovers tend to be women with careers and incomes that make a gift of a necklace exactly that. A gift. A token of affection."

She swallowed, hyperaware that her motion caused the edge of his thumb to brush her skin. She drew back enough to release her hair from his touch, disturbed by the thought of his having lovers. Rich, powerful lovers for whom he had affection. She probably knew some of them.

"I'm not clear on what you need compensation for. And why you think it's up to me to provide it."

"Your cousin sold me a pile of useless rocks, not the rare metals he led me to expect would fuel the next generation of my electronic devices." His muted fury was contained, but instant. Volatile and very real. A glimpse into the volcano vent.

Her fingers tightened on the stem of her glass and she stood very still. "Surely you know that mining is as much a gamble as any slot machine in Vegas."

"The Barsi name on the original test results carried a lot of weight. Heavy hitters signed on. When the mine didn't pay out as advertised, the investors insisted on fresh samples.

They were duds. I've had to lock up much of my operating capital in an escrow account while I wait out the investigation. It's costing me daily to carry all that risk and debt. If Benny doesn't show up and clear my name, I lose that money and pay fines on top of it—which could cost me *everything*."

She didn't dare ask if he was the one who had misrepresented or exaggerated test samples. He wouldn't be so inimical if he didn't have an ax to grind. She felt helpless in the face of everything he was saying, desperate to defuse the situation.

"I swear to you, Benny wouldn't deliberately mislead anyone about something like that. Was there some other go-between?"

"I was dealing with him directly." His cheeks went hollow as he penetrated her with laser eyes. "And I believe your family also invests heavily in precious metals. No doubt gains have been made on your more-established fronts since this new opportunity has fallen through."

She gasped with outrage. "Are you suggesting we're deliberately manipulating prices with supply and demand? No! We would never do anything like that."

"I'm sure you wouldn't blacklist me in New York, either."

"Of course not!"

"Yet whispers are circulating loud enough that no one in New York is returning my calls. Damage is being done that won't stop until Benny resurfaces. I think I deserve compensation for that, Gisella. Don't you?"

Her insides felt cold and heavy, chilling her with dread. She threw up her hands in helplessness. "I didn't know any of this!"

His lip curled with contempt, telling her she could talk herself blue. In his mind, the evidence was stacked too high against all of them.

She looked to her phone, desperately willing Benny to call and make all of this go away. All she wanted was a single earring, for heaven's sake. How had this gone so horribly wrong?

"Who did you call earlier?" Kaine asked.

"Benny's father. He's heard the rumors, but there's nothing we can do except not repeat them."

"You can stop trying to take further advantage of me."

"I'm not! *We* are not."

"Why are you here, then? Dressed to do business," he added in a disparaging tone.

"I dressed to get into your lousy party!" Truly lousy, although, as insults went, it wasn't her best.

"And our kiss at the estate auction? Is that a charming New York custom I'm unaware of? Have I been missing out by settling for handshakes instead of the five alarm fire you offered?"

"Oh, for—!" She rolled her eyes to the ceiling, glad for the low light because she was so hot she must be blushing all the way into her cleavage. "I was attracted to you so I kissed you. Is that so hard to believe?"

"That passion was real?" he mocked. "Come here, then." He set aside his glass with a clink on a glass tabletop. "Let's finish what we started."

"God, you're overbearing!" She closed her fists, but managed to keep them at her side.

His wolfish gaze wasn't what scared her, though. *He* wasn't. It was herself and the stupid impulse in her feet that had nearly carried her forward on his command to do exactly what he said that terrified her. She still wanted to see. To *feel*.

"I went to the auction for an earring. I kissed a man who interested me. I've since realized what a mistake that was."

"It was," he agreed. "A big one." He picked up his drink again, adding in a smooth, lethal tone, "I have half a mind to accept Rohan's latest offer just to punish you."

"Don't," she said through gritted teeth, telling herself she shouldn't be shocked at how vindictive and ruthless he was. She'd already seen him in action.

He smirked. "It's amazing how quickly that little sparkler brings you to heel. I'm starting to think it has a cold war spy transmitter in it that's still active."

"I'm starting to think this sounds like extortion. Why are you being so heavy-handed?"

"So that you understand all that's at stake as we discuss terms."

She shifted, uncomfortable, and folded her arms. "What exactly are you asking me to do, then?"

"You're adorable. I'm not asking. I'm telling you that, starting now, you're going to portray yourself as my latest and most smitten lover." He savored that pronouncement with a sip of wine that he seemed to roll around on his tongue.

"Oh, so you *blackmail* women into your bed."

For a moment, he didn't move. Neither did she, fearing she'd gone too far. But did he hear himself? As the silence prolonged, she began to feel hemmed in and trapped. Far too close to him. Suffocated.

"The fact you didn't hear the word *portray* says more about your desires than mine," he mocked softly. He was full out laughing in silence at her. *So* overbearing.

"I won't be blackmailed into playing pretend, either," she stated. "Why would you even want me to?"

He sobered. "If I'm being accused of trying to cheat investors, I want it known that I wasn't acting alone. I'm firmly in bed with the Barsi family."

"No. We can't let people believe we had anything to do with someone accused of fraud." It had taken three generations of honest business to build Barsi on Fifth into its current, iconic status. Rumors of imitations and deceit could tear it down overnight.

"Oh, I should let myself continue to be your patsy?"

Her shaky composure dropped another notch, but she clung to it with her fingernails. "Whatever power you think you have over me, you don't. Go ahead and sell the earring. I don't care," she lied.

"Please. You have so many pressure points, I don't have enough fingers to reach them all.

The earring is the most expedient, but you have a cousin trying get into Juilliard, don't you? Your mother's tenure isn't bulletproof. Nor is your aunt and uncle's mortgage. Did you know there's a database vulnerability at Barsi on Fifth? Certain clients would be mortified if their purchase records were hacked and published."

"That's illegal!"

"I didn't say I would do it. But a rumor that it could happen would repel a good portion of your customer base—the mistress-keepers and politicians."

"You're a horrible person."

"I'm a man who strikes back when he's double-crossed. Either you lift me up, or I take you down."

"Generous as your offer to become your fake dalliance sounds, I have a job and a life in New York."

"One into which you are eager to introduce your new lover."

"That is a ridiculous—" Well, it was hardly a request, was it? "—demand."

"I can't let my reputation deteriorate while I wait for your cousin to reappear and explain himself," Kaine said in an uncompromising tone. "Especially if that explanation still leaves me looking like the one who orchestrated the fraud. I need to start rebuilding my name. And I want an inside track on your family while I do it, keeping an eye on every move you and your family make, especially as it pertains to my interests. If you really believe your cousin is innocent, you'll want to limit the damage he's caused me. Because I make a terrible enemy."

"I've noticed," she bit out.

"Then we have an agreement."

Oh, she hated that presumptive tone in his voice. She also hated the edgy restlessness invading her. She ought to be repulsed, but latent biological tremors were shivering through her. She shouldn't want to spend more time with him, let alone feel a certain relief that she had an excuse to.

The very fact she had all these conflicting feelings told her she ought to run far and fast, but he *was* a terrible enemy. She had witnessed his iron-hard single-mindedness herself the day of the estate auction. If he threw that kind of money and fury directly at Barsi on Fifth, they might weather the storm, but not without suffering near-catastrophic damage.

Ultimately, that's what swung her decision: family. Her own grandmother had made a painful sacrifice to give her the life she enjoyed. Gisella could make a small one to mitigate damage to her clan. But—

"How long is this supposed to go on?"

"Until your cousin shows up to explain himself. I'm sure you'll be motivated to make that happen within a few weeks."

"Fine," she said. "I'll do it. But I won't sleep with you."

"If I was trying to seduce you, you'd know it," he taunted, then sobered. "And if you think you can seduce me…" He dipped his chin so they were nearly eye to eye, so she could see how serious and lethal he was. "It's important you understand that I invest in games, Gisella. I don't play them. If you slide that silky body into my bed trying to get something—"

"I won't," she swore, heart slamming with sudden emotion. Anticipation? Guilt?

"You will," he said darkly. "At some point, you'll want something. The earring, leniency, something. And you'll do it. But be warned. I'll take whatever you offer, but I won't give you anything in return. Except orgasms," he drawled. "I try to be generous on that front."

His words, the way his lips and tongue caressed her name, were a sensual punch in her midsection even as her heart twisted at his view of her.

All she could manage, however, was a weak, "I'll have to take your word for it."

"Then we have a deal."

CHAPTER FOUR

A KNOCK WOKE HER. "Breakfast is here."

Gisella opened her eyes to brilliant sunshine bouncing off creamy walls. She hadn't closed the navy-colored blinds last night, staring across the city well after Kaine had insisted she cancel her reservation and stay in his guest room.

She'd been tired enough by the time shift to accept and had locked herself in here for a bath and a brood.

Now her eyes felt gritty, her brain sluggish. She rolled onto her back and snuggled the soft bamboo sheets to her chin, tempted to stay in this bed forever. But it was eight o'clock. Eleven in New York.

The lamp shade over the clock was a tranquil aqua to match the accent pillow on the chair. Other than that, there was no furniture, just a mirrored wall that hid the closet and reflected the view of the bay along with her pale, unblinking face.

She forced herself out of bed, took extra care with her appearance so he wouldn't be able to tell she'd had a hellish night and descended to the main floor, where he sat on the veranda in the sun. It was exactly as tranquil as she had pictured when she had first seen this place last night.

He was reading his phone, dishes still covered while he waited for her. He wore pajama bottoms, a T-shirt and bare feet. He gave her corduroy capris and sleeveless top a look that said, *Meh.* "Wrong message. And winter is over."

"Get a lot of paparazzi photos up here, do you?"

"Drones are a thing. But start as you mean to go on, is what I'm saying." He set aside his phone.

"In your case, overbearing and judgmental?" She sat and reached to pour a cup of coffee.

He offered his own for a top up, then lifted the tray covers. "Remarks like that will remain between us. It will be our thing."

"If you insist. Darling," she agreed with a smarmy smile, tilting her cup in a small salute on the way to her lips.

His sharp gaze snagged on the flash of her ring in the sunlight. His expression changed. "Did you make that?"

It shouldn't surprise her that he knew what she did for a living. He had said he did his homework and she had read up online about him. Even so, his question wasn't idle. He seemed genuinely interested, which set her on her back foot as she answered.

"My cousin did."

"May I?" He held out a hand for hers.

She set down her cup, always willing to show off the stunning art deco piece with its arrangement of tapered baguettes, but his touch caused a quick leap in her blood that made her give a tiny jerk.

He glanced at her, expression not changing, but she sensed a radiation of satisfaction. He used his thumb to center what was already a precisely balanced platinum setting on her middle finger. His touch barely grazed her skin, but still felt like a caress.

"A family tradition or something?" He didn't let go when he lifted his gaze again.

"A graduation gift. Rozi and I are the only goldsmiths in this generation." It took all her concentration to ignore the way the tingling in her hand intensified as he continued to hold it. "We were inspired by the family business and apprenticed under our uncle Ben, Benny's father. As we were finishing up, he had us make a ring for each other. It was an exercise of sorts, to prove we were ready to work on commission. When you're making custom pieces for other people, you have to think more about what they would like to wear, less about what you want to make."

"Is this something you *would* make for yourself?"

No one had ever asked her that. She cocked her head.

"Probably not. Rozi picked the stones to

represent her and our five cousins. It's a sentimental act I wouldn't think to do for myself. As a gift, however, it's extremely thoughtful."

"You're the diamond," he guessed, still holding her hand.

"It's a white sapphire, but yes. She's the rose-colored one. Rozalia." Obviously. "The yellow and blue and green are the boys. The red and purple are the other girls."

"It ought to be garish, but it's really quite beautiful." He shifted her hand to make it catch the light.

"She knew I would go crazy for the design, so she put the work in. If you knew how fussy you have to be when setting the stones to achieve those angles, you'd be even more impressed."

"You sound fond of her."

"She's another pressure point, yes. If that's what you're asking," Gisella said, disdainfully pulling her hand free. "I adore all my cousins, but Rozi and I are the same age. We were inseparable growing up. I love this ring, but the fact it's made by her is what makes it extra special. Feel free to steal it if you ever want me to kill you outright."

"So dramatic." His mouth twitched. "What did you make for her?"

She reached for her phone, trying not to be self-conscious as she flicked through her portfolio album. Why was she attacked by nerves? She was proud of every single piece she'd ever made. Rozi adored the ring she'd given her.

She showed him the photo of a rose gold band of vine leaves. Some glistened with diamonds as dewdrops. Others were shaped to protectively cup the black opal at the center.

"The photo doesn't do justice to the colors in the stone." Even so, it wasn't as flashy as the ring she wore. She felt a sudden need to defend that choice. "Rozi is very feminine and in touch with nature's rhythms. When people meet her, they often underestimate her. She calls herself 'garden variety,' but she's tenacious and resilient and has depths you don't see right away."

"It's beautiful."

Was he being truthful? She couldn't tell and didn't understand why she wanted him to like it. He was a layman and couldn't possibly appreciate the love and meticulous care she had taken to perfect that ring.

"Thank you," she murmured, taking back her phone. "She's—"

She hesitated. Everything with this man felt like she was inching onto a gangplank. She couldn't tell if honesty was the best policy or a future pitfall, but she wanted him to believe her only reason for coming here was the earring, not some covert operation for Benny. She certainly didn't want Rozi's whereabouts to come out later and be misinterpreted.

"Rozi is in Hungary." She helped herself to the spinach and smoked salmon topped with poached egg. "She's making an offer to Viktor Rohan for his earring as we speak." If all was going according to plan. Dear God, she hoped things hadn't gone off the rails as badly for her cousin as they had for her.

Kaine sat back. "What do you know about him?"

"Besides the fact he's my cousin?"

That caught his attention, which made her want to say, Ha!

"I thought you do your homework," she murmured in a soft taunt.

"So you're here on his behalf." His lip curled in distaste.

"No," she dismissed with an exasperated, "Tsk." Honestly, he made her sound like a double agent. "I've never even met him or bothered learning anything about that side of my family until Rozi discovered he had Grandmamma's other earring. Mom and I have always regarded Benedek Senior as Mom's father. Mom believed it until she typed her blood in science class when she was fourteen. That's when Grandmamma had to explain that Mom's biological father had died before Mom was born. His name was Istvan. We never really talked much about it beyond that."

"How does Rohan's family come to have it?"

"That's one of the questions Rozi will be sure to ask while she's there. It sounds like their family has old money. They could have bought it anytime in the last fifty years."

"Rohan is extremely well connected and determined. *Very* deep pockets."

"Is that a warning?"

"A question. I don't understand why you and your cousin are going up against someone like him—or me—for a bauble that sits in a drawer unworn because you have to be Van Gogh to only want one earring."

She sputtered on a laugh. "That's terrible," she admonished.

He shrugged. "Rohan made it clear to me he's acquiring, not selling. I understand his perspective. It's like compiling a vertical of vintage wines. The value is in owning the pair. You said yourself it's not that valuable and the appraiser I hired agreed. He said the stones are good quality and the setting is twenty-two karats, but a similar piece made today would sell for a few thousand dollars. Ten thousand for the set, tops."

"I wouldn't go that low," she said with disdain. "It sounds like your appraiser is giving little weight to the craftsmanship in hand-cutting the stones or the granulations process with the setting. That's very technical for the late eighteen hundreds, when only a handful of goldsmiths knew how to do it. I'm dying to hold the earring just for the chance to study the artistry."

She sent him a pointed look.

"Keep handing me these pressure points, darling. I'm happy to keep using them." He bit the tip off a spear of grilled asparagus.

The food was excellent, not that she was paying much attention, far too caught up in the conversation and him. He was incredibly sexy in his casual wear and stubble and giving her all his attention this way. Her heart tremored and her bones softened just holding his gaze.

If she wasn't careful, she would forget that she had told him she wouldn't sleep with him. She would forget how important it was to prove him wrong about her. She cleared her throat.

"The value for *us* is sentimental. We want to give the earrings back to Grandmamma. They were all she had of Istvan. It broke her heart to lose him. She didn't even get to keep the one she brought to America. She had to sell it when she ran out of money."

"She was married to Barsi when she arrived in New York."

"No. She was alone and pregnant. She had my mother a few months after arriving. I can't imagine how lonely and desperate she must have felt. She went to Grandpapa to sell the ring. He felt sorry for her and offered to marry her in exchange for the right. He sold it to open the shop."

"They came to America as husband and wife." He sounded so confident, it gave her the tiniest niggle of doubt, but she knew her family history and got her back up.

"People have made that assumption before, but no. Grandmamma knew Grandpapa from Budapest. She sold the first earring to him there. He unloaded it right away because he was liquidating to emigrate, too. People were fleeing in droves. They wound up on the same ship, but it was coincidence. When she ran out of money from the first earring, she tracked him down in New York and sold him the second one. He was quite a bit older than her, but he was starting his own shop. He needed help on his counter. She asked for a job, but given her circumstance with a new baby, he offered to marry her. They pooled their resources. It started as a marriage of convenience, but she grew to love him. It's a very sweet story."

"It would be, if it were true." The look he gave her wasn't so much patronizing as amused, as though he thought it laughable she believed what she was saying. "I had an investigator compile a report on Benny before I met you, when I first realized things were going sideways with his claims about the mine's payout. The report states your grandfather came over with his wife, Eszti Barsi. They shared a cabin. Your mother still uses that name."

"Because Benedek Barsi is the only father she knew." Did he listen *at all*? "But Grandmamma and Grandpapa didn't marry until Grandmamma had been here several months. I *know* that."

"How?"

"Because she told me!"

"I was given the original bill of sale on the New York earring as part of its pedigree. The Garrison widow bought it in the fall of 1956, almost immediately after your grandparents arrived, not months after the ship docked. Old man Barsi used the first earring to finance their passage as husband and wife. Then they used the money from the sale of the second one to set up the shop in New York."

"Your investigator is wrong." She was growing contentious now. "My grandmother wouldn't lie about something so big."

"Your family only tells small lies?"

"We don't lie at all!"

"Except tiny white ones like listing the wrong father on a birth certificate and letting your mother believe it for fourteen years. Or, perhaps, a little white lie to investors about the quality of a mining sample."

"I just explained that Grandmamma was a desperate woman in a difficult situation. It's not like today, when women can just get pregnant and raise a baby on their own if they want to. Can I see this bill of sale?"

"It's in the safe-deposit box with the earring. The auction agency was told that Mrs. Garrison bought the earring thinking she could have a match made, or could break up the setting and reuse the stones and melt down the gold."

Gisella cringed at the suggestion.

"But the setting was too complex and the stones were difficult to match. She offered more than once to sell it back to Barsi, or exchange it for something else. Your grandfather wouldn't give her the price she wanted."

"You are *so* wrong. My grandparents never knew where the earrings wound up. They would have told us. Rozalia and I have been trying to find the earrings for years."

He barely flicked an eyebrow at that. "They

might not have known where the first one went, but they knew where the New York one was."

"Can I see this report you've compiled on *my* family?"

"Pay for your own," he said mildly.

She set her jaw. "Perhaps I'll pay for one on *you*. How would you like that? Me, snooping into *your* background, making judgments and false claims?"

He shrugged. "Since my family history is about two hundred and forty characters long, and already online, I'll save you the time and trouble. I never knew my father, my mother died when I was young, and I spent more time in juvenile detention than foster homes—shoplifting, mostly, but also petty vandalism and fighting. When I turned sixteen, I got a job with a landscape company that needed a strong back on a shovel. I started saving for my own truck, wanting to work for myself. Three years later, I was under a client's balcony when I overheard him talking someone into investing in his latest start-up. He was convinced there'd be a windfall within six months. I gambled my savings and quadrupled it a few months later. I decided I no longer wanted to work for myself. I wanted people to work for me. Judge away."

Gisella blinked, taking apart all he had said in such a matter-of-fact tone, wanting more than that succinct report when he must have had deep feelings about some of it. What sorts of scars had it left on him that he hid under his air of imperviousness?

"Did you ever try to find your father?"

"I don't know his name."

"What about your oh-so-competent investigator? Can't he help?"

"My mother didn't book passage on a ship. Her great-grandparents walked in from Mexico and married Texans. Their descendants are in San Diego—and elsewhere by now, I imagine—but I've never tried to form ties."

Something in his stoic delivery struck her, but the impression was gone before she could analyze it.

"She came north quite young, likely with

my father when she was pregnant. He might have been in the military, but that's uncon-firmed. If she ever told me anything about him, I was too young to remember it."

"How old were you when you lost her?"

"Five."

"And you went into foster care? Didn't they try to contact her family on your behalf?"

"They were struggling, unable to take on a child they didn't know."

He wasn't betraying any reaction, making all of this sound very factual, but she thought she saw the tiniest flash of an old fury in his unwavering gaze.

"I'm sorry."

"Foster care wasn't that bad." His shoul-der jerked in a negligent shrug. "If I'd had an ounce of sense, I would have stayed out of trouble and remained there. Juvey sucks. At least the experience of incarceration keeps me honest as an adult. That, and having enough money that I don't have to resort to criminal behavior when I want something."

She imagined he was referring to what he

thought Benny had done, but she ignored it, too caught up in what sounded like a very lonely childhood.

"You don't have any siblings? No family at all?"

"*You* don't have any siblings," he pointed out. "Shall I pity you?" His lip curled with amused disdain at what must be showing in her face.

"I don't pity you. I empathize. I've *always* wanted a brother or sister."

"Why? You have all these cousins you adore."

"True. But they all had siblings. I felt cheated, being an only child." She sipped her coffee. "I suppose if I was completely honest, I should admit they treated me like a sibling, especially Rozi. I grew up in her house. Both of my parents worked and Rozi's mom, my aunt Agotha, was a homemaker. I went to her every weekday morning, before we left for school. I came back there with my cousins when the bell rang and only went to my own home when Mom or Dad picked me up after dinner. I resented going home to an empty room, though. When I was allowed to have sleepovers, I was in heaven."

"The sleepovers I can understand," he said drily. "I enjoy them myself."

"I—" She almost said she wouldn't know, but caught herself. "Well, I suppose you'll have to curtail those, now you're enamored with me." She smiled sweetly.

"My door is always open. I'll just put that out there."

"I won't put out at all," she said firmly, and made the mistake of trying to stare him down.

As their gazes stayed locked, a visceral and very pleasurable wave of sensuality seeped into her. It felt like a submission of sorts, but it was different. She wasn't cowed. He wasn't scaring her. Rather, some biological reaction was making her pliant as she contemplated sleeping with him. He was an alpha in his prime. Her body gave off signals of welcome and reciprocity without her conscious desire to do so. She saw him grow more alert as he became aware of it. He seemed to become bigger, not in a threatening way, yet threatening to overwhelm.

Her breathing changed. Her eyes grew damp. She forced her gaze to the blue-on-blue horizon.

"How are we supposed to act enthralled with each other when we can't stand one another?"

"Is that true? I could have sworn we just had a moment."

"Oh, I see. You're delusional." She flicked a crumb off her knee.

His teeth flashed as he bit the corner off a triangle of sourdough toast.

"This banter of yours intrigues me. It's a defense mechanism, but why? Because you know I'm on to you? Or because you're genuinely attracted to me and uncomfortable with it? Why would that bother you? Because you're not in control of your reaction? Or can't manipulate mine?"

The inability to control her reaction was exactly the problem, but she didn't want to admit it.

"Do you have any sleepover companions you'll have to dismiss?" His inquiry came off as idle, but the air shimmered, loaded with sexual tension and something more dangerous.

"Not at the moment, no." Never. Why did that make her blush?

"We'll see if we cave to deprivation, then." He was laughing at her behind those watchful, cast-in-bronze eyes.

"Is that how it works for you?" She flashed him an annoyed glance. "A timer goes off behind your fly, indicating you're due for a close encounter?"

"I meet a woman whose company I enjoy and things progress from there."

"Whew." She swept a mocking hand across her brow. "Guess I'll be able to dodge that bullet."

"Oh, you're making this highly enjoyable and you know it. For the record, I'm not smug when I win. There won't be any I-told-you-so when you wake up in my bed."

"Brace yourself for my victory dance when

I don't. I'm competitive and annoying when *I* win."

"My ego can take it."

He tried to snag her gaze again, but she didn't let him, choosing to concentrate on smoothing jam on her sourdough instead.

"Tell me about your social scene in New York," he said after a moment. "I expect you're in high demand. I want a full calendar from the moment we arrive."

"Good luck with that." She made a face. "I don't accept many invitations, especially to parties or, worse, fundraisers. I make a donation and don't waste my time showing up."

"Why is it a waste of time? That depends on your goals, doesn't it? What are yours?"

"When I go to a social event? To say hello to friends or family. I enjoy dancing, but you can't dance with a man without him thinking you want to go home with him. And I'm not interested in casual hookups," she stated firmly, because it had always been true. "I'm where I want to be career-wise, so I'm not trying to impress someone or network my way into a promotion. The only reason to go out is social and I'm choosy about whom I spend my time with. Why? What are your goals?"

"None of those things, either. I'm exactly where I want to be, as well."

She bet he was, nursing coffee at the top of his tower every morning, able to see to Hawaii from here.

"But I learn a lot about human behavior and what people need when they're in social gatherings. They reveal the minutiae of their lives, which helps me evaluate the pitches I receive. Games and other entertainments can be lucrative, but people also want useful technology. Something that gives back while giving them something. So I listen. Are we saving the whales these days? Or the rain forest? Organizing carpools? Or curating newsfeeds? What are people crying out for?"

"That sounds cold-blooded, tying random do-good causes into selling whatever service is trending."

"That's business." He shrugged. "Do you want to play a game that shows you cascading jewels? Or open an app that provides current trading prices on precious gems while putting a share of profits back into the fair trade process of mining them?"

"Point to you. In fact, send me a link if that app actually exists."

"It was off the top of my head. Give me a week, though. I'll have a beta version you can test." He picked up his phone and spoke a memo into it.

She didn't want to admire him for his slick ease at providing something she hadn't even known she desired. She didn't want to like him period, but his lazy confidence and sexy repartee was exhilarating.

"Jewelry used to give back while giving," she mused, warming her coffee with a top-up. "Men gave their wives rings and necklaces as a token of affection, but it was also a status symbol and acted as a savings account or insurance policy. She had a means to support herself and their children if something happened to him. Families used to give watches and pendants to commemorate graduations and other milestones. Now the children get a tablet or a game station—which are redundant within a few years."

"The children?"

"You know what I mean."

"If you believe that, why go into making jewelry yourself?"

"Because it's art and science. Challenging, but pretty." She shrugged at the thrill she got from playing with gold and sparkling gems. "People never complain about how much they spend, either. They're happy because they feel like they get back something that will appreciate when everything else you buy these days is disposable. And it makes people happy to adorn themselves. I can put a new clasp on a necklace for five dollars and they're smiling the rest of the day."

"Which makes me wonder about your grandmother's earring. You're willing to pay more than it's worth to anyone else, so it won't appreciate. And how is it useful to her at this stage? Say what you will about technology, but if you want to enhance an old memory for her, you could do it far more effectively by making an album of her childhood haunts. All of Hungary is on your phone."

"That's nostalgia. The earring is a symbol of *love*."

"I don't have your vast experience of such a thing, of course," he said scathingly. "But that particular emotion seems the epitome of useless."

She possessed a certain cynicism where romantic love was concerned. Even so, his scorn stung, making her look to the side and blink hot eyes. It was as if he found the deepest, most secretive part of her and laughed at it. She *wanted* to believe in love, needed to believe it would be hers one day. Her grandmother's earring was one of the few solid pieces of evidence she had that it existed.

"At best, love gives back obligation or pain," he continued. "You love your family and where has that got you?"

Here. With him.

She looked down at her plate, heart so exposed and raw, she swore it must be visible in the base of her throat.

Because it wasn't just love for her family that pinned her in this chair. She was here because she wanted to know more about him. He drew her in ways she couldn't explain even to herself. She wanted to chip past the dark, gnarled edges on him and see what facets could be revealed underneath.

"You're right that it doesn't matter how skillful the setting, a pile of polished stones isn't going to fix Grandmamma's broken heart. But she'll see the action for what it is—a desire to alleviate her pain. That's what love is. A cushion and a balm. A shield. That's why I'm here. I want to absorb or deflect the pain that might otherwise hit the rest of my family if I don't cooperate with you."

"You don't care what that costs you?" He shook his head as though she was a lost cause.

"I do care. I know it will cost me." She lifted her chin and leveled her gaze into his turbulent bronze one. "But I'm willing to do it anyway. *That's* what love is."

* * *

They arrived to a late spring squall in New York. The rain spat at them sideways across the tarmac, reminding Kaine why he lived in California. He lifted open the edge of his jacket to shield Gisella as they hurried down the stairs of his private jet and trotted across the tarmac toward his limousine.

She fit perfectly into his side, warm and lithe and sweet smelling, tugging all the latent desire he'd been fighting through the flight fully back to life.

He'd had a restless night, expecting her to come to him. He had willed her to, even though he still doubted her motives. She had seemed genuinely surprised about her cousin's duplicity, yet seemed equally determined to take the hit for it—which didn't make sense to him. Loyalty went only so far. Definitely familial loyalty was a fickle thing. *He* hadn't been on the receiving end of any when he'd needed it.

As for love? He had confused sexual infatuation for that emotion once. It had cost him an engagement ring, a handful of company secrets and a streak of red in his bank balance.

So his ability to trust Gisella was a tank on empty. He found it awfully coincidental that she had piqued his interest so acutely at the auction, then arrived like a gift as his patience with her cousin was growing thin. She was a Trojan horse. Had to be.

Which meant he shouldn't be dragging her into his life the way he was.

Sexual infatuation had a firm grip on his libido, though. He had it in his head that he could let her play out her game and come to his bed when she thought that move would serve her purpose. At that point, he would strike a deal and quench this fire.

Until then, he had to be patient—which wasn't easy. The downpour did nothing to ease the desire burning in him and she was utterly breathtaking with her face damp and flushed as though in the throes of passion.

"Do you not drive?" she asked as she accepted a hand towel he dug from behind a sliding panel in the back of the limo. She patted her face, ensuring her makeup remained unsmudged.

"Not in the city. I can be more productive in the backseat."

She glanced at him with suspicion.

He smirked. "You heard that. I didn't say it."

Her long lashes swept dismissively, trying to act disgusted, but her mouth twitched.

That was what was getting to him. He didn't know how that sort of sexual awareness could be faked, so he wanted to believe it was real.

He had to stay on guard, though. She was inordinately beautiful, captivating even, but also smart and tough. Adding a sense of humor to that package was cashmere carpets in a Ferrari, taking high performance to a luxury level that made a man want to stay inside it forever.

And, yeah, he was well aware of the double entendre in *that*, but, oh, it was true.

"I own several cars that I drive myself when I can get out on the highways." He almost added, *I'll let you pick the color and direction next time I do.* Running along a coastal highway with the radio blaring, top down so her hair whipped around her beautiful face, would make for a great start to a long, sexy weekend.

But she wasn't his lover.

Yet, a dark voice whispered in the back of his head, making his scalp prickle with anticipation. He ran the towel over his wet hair, erasing the tingles along with his erotic fantasies, determined to bide his time. His standing and net worth had been damaged enough by her cousin. If he allowed lust to blind him, he could lose everything and he would *not* go back to zero.

He asked her to give her address to the driver and did what he'd done during the flight across the country—used work as a distraction, doing his best to ignore the sexual undercurrents trying to sweep him away.

Gisella couldn't fault his work ethic. Kaine had been tied up through the flight and made a call as they drove to Manhattan. He often spoke in Spanish, which she had told him she understood, but he didn't seem to care if she eavesdropped. This latest call wasn't a hot stock tip or anything, just a boring restructuring discussion anyway.

"Do you have offices here?" she asked when he ended his call.

"As of this morning, yes. I also have footprints in Vancouver, Sydney and London. Establishing a base here was scheduled to happen sooner, but recent events caused me to be shut out of certain real estate markets."

She heard the censure in his remark and bit her lip, but had to insist, "We don't have that sort of influence with real estate firms."

"No. One of my investors was trying to put pressure on me. It's surprising how quickly he backed down once I bought the Garrison mansion out from under him."

"Mr. Walters?"

"Yes. And I'm quite the belle of the ball with the real estate brokers now. Had my pick of the snobbiest street numbers. Speaking of elite neighborhoods…" Kaine dipped his head to study the brownstone as his driver parked in the no-parking zone on her tree-lined boulevard. "Is this where you live?"

"With my mother, yes." That sounded so juvenile, she had to explain. "When my parents divorced, Dad put his half in my name. Mom and I own it together. I don't see the point in paying rent elsewhere."

She watched him lean to take in the decorative wrought iron rails that enclosed the wide entrance steps, complete with a gate across them. The street-level windows of their lower floor were protected with matching wrought iron bars behind a waist-high fence. Well-tended shrubs and newly planted spring flowers softened the otherwise minimal and geometrical facade.

"Good thing I secured us alternate accommodation. I have no desire to live with your mother."

"Us?"

"Of course. We're a couple. Is she home? I'll come in and meet her while you pack."

"I thought you were dropping me off! Do

you seriously expect me to go in there and tell my mother I'm moving in with you?"

"Look at you, blushing like a virgin." His gaze caressed her hot cheeks, making them sting all the harder. "Does she not know what the rest of the family is up to?" His gaze turned to hammered bronze.

"We're not up to anything and she'll be surprised because I don't bring men home!"

For more reasons than one. Gisella loved her mother, but their relationship wasn't conventional. Certainly not the iconic one Rozi had with *her* mother. That intractable warmth and affection was another reason she had always envied her cousins. Her mother was more inclined to critique than support and wasn't effusive at all. The few men she had introduced to her had *not* been worth her mother's time and she'd let Gisella know it.

The driver opened the door. She couldn't leave him standing there, getting soaked, while holding an umbrella for her. She threw herself from the car and scooted through the gate with a practiced twist of her wrist on the clasp.

Kaine trotted up the stairs alongside her, holding the umbrella over her. He crowded into the covered space on the stoop, where he shook the water off the umbrella and closed it.

The limousine pulled away with a hiss of tires on wet pavement.

Gisella punched the code into the security panel, mentally urging the lock to release since Kaine's presence beside her was far too overwhelming. She had been aware of him all through the flight, then beside her in the car. Standing this close, she could feel the heat radiating off him from his open jacket and smell the subtle scent of his aftershave. The way he took command of her senses was as thought-scattering as the rest of his imperious grasp on her life.

"It's me," Gisella called as they entered, since her aunt and a few other family members also came and went with the touch of a few buttons. "Are you home?"

"Marking," her mother answered from beyond the open door of her study. "I thought you were away all weekend."

"Change of plans." Gisella glanced at Kaine.

He was taking in the immaculate foyer and pristine living room. Period pieces in blue velvet and mahogany were arranged with an oxblood sofa facing an intricately carved mantel over a fireplace that hadn't been lit in decades. Another arch in the far wall led to the dining area, where the back wall of the house had been opened into a succession of tall windows and French doors onto a small veranda. It looked onto a renovated carriage house. Their renter kept a tiny vegetable garden in the courtyard between, making it a pleasant place to sit when the weather was better.

"Can you come out?" Gisella moved to the door on the other side of the foyer and found her mother exactly as she'd seen her a million times—at her desk with a red-inked pen in hand. "I have Kaine Michaels with me. I'd like to introduce you."

"That man from the auction you were so angry with? Why is he here?"

Gisella bit back a sigh. Her mother was an academic with a passion for the broad strokes of history, not troubling herself too much with the subtler dynamics of one-on-one interpersonal relationships.

At the same time, she had firm beliefs on how women ought to conduct themselves so Gisella took a small, bracing breath before announcing, "I'll be staying with him while he's in New York."

"Oh?" Her mother lifted her head. Her eyes appeared owlish behind her glasses. "Why is that?"

Gisella smiled flatly. "For the same reason most women stay with a man, Mom."

Her mother put down her pen and took off her glasses. "I thought you had an agreement with Rozi. Does this mean you're serious about him?"

"No." She was aware of Kaine a few feet away, able to hear every word they exchanged, which made this extra mortifying. "But we'd like to see where it goes."

She could practically hear Kaine's disparaging thoughts about her ability to lie.

"Giving up your independence is a terrible way to start any relationship. I've told you that a hundred times." Ah, her mother the bra burner.

"I live with my mother," Gisella reminded. "There's not much independence to give up. And this is a decision I'm making for myself." Another lie. Kaine had very much made it for her. "I only came to introduce you and grab a few things. Will you come out and meet him?"

"I suppose," her mother murmured, rising. A moment later, Gisella made the introduction.

Have fun, she silently conveyed to Kaine as she went upstairs to pack.

Kaine wasn't sure what he had expected, but Alisz Barsi wasn't it.

She was older than he anticipated, early

sixties, likely. She wore a dove-gray sweater set over a pair of flowing black pants and no makeup. Her hair was a faded version of Gisella's caramel and shot with streaks of silver. She carried an air of elegant confidence that didn't intimidate him, but ensured he knew she wasn't intimidated *by* him. Probably not by any man, woman or beast on this earth.

Like mother, like daughter, he thought drily.

He welcomed the chance to sit with her, however. Not just for the glimpse into the Barsi dynasty, but to see inside Gisella's childhood, the one she had spoken of in a way that had almost sounded as lonely as his, despite her tight circle of extended family.

He had identified with Gisella's longing for siblings. As a young child, he had felt untethered and wished for closer connections. Later relationships had taught him it was far better to rely only on himself. These days, he was comfortable living a solo, but he was still curious how the other half lived.

Alisz ordered coffee from a housekeeper.

They talked about their respective jobs while they drank it. If she knew anything about her nephew's fraud, she didn't let on. She hadn't gone into the family business, she said, because she preferred to study history. She had authored several textbooks and other papers with a focus on elevating the forgotten women who had contributed to advancements over the centuries.

She likened his line of work and the current technological revolution to the industrial and agricultural revolutions of the past, cautioning him to allow women their share in the glory. He assured her that he actively worked toward gender balance in the workplace.

He couldn't tell one way or another if Alisz approved of his relationship with her daughter, which was a new experience. More than one middle-aged CEO or venture capitalist had tried to introduce her daughter to him, recognizing the secure future he represented. He didn't enjoy being stalked like fresh meat by women twice his age, but he was used to it.

Alisz wasn't measuring him for a groom's

tuxedo at all. On the contrary, he got the impression she regarded him as a phase and was being polite only for her daughter's sake. Was this why Gisella didn't bring men home?

Why did he care?

He didn't, he assured himself.

"Kaine was just telling me you have an engagement and can't stay for dinner," her mother said when Gisella returned to the lounge.

Gisella's expression fell into a neutral poker face. "I told Dad I would be in San Francisco and miss Susan's fortieth, but since we're here, I'll take this opportunity to introduce them."

"Ah. Wish Susan many happy returns for me." She sipped her coffee and set it aside. If she resented her ex-husband's new wife, it didn't show in her tone or expression.

"Ready?" Kaine rose.

Gisella hesitated, then said, "One quick question, Mom."

She directed a stalwart smile toward her mother as the older woman rose and faced her.

"Kaine's paperwork on Grandmamma's earring says the Garrisons purchased it as soon as she arrived in New York. He was told they tried to sell it back to Grandpapa, but he didn't want it."

Her mother made a face that dismissed pesky details.

"It was your uncle who fielded the offer. He asked me if I wanted it, but Papa was still alive. I thought it would be disrespectful to take it. Besides, what would I do with one earring? I declined."

"You could have given it to Grandmamma. She loved your father, Mom."

"Her feelings toward my father are not mine." She gave an indifferent shrug. "My connection to Istvan has never meant anything to me. It would have been even more hurtful to Papa to give it to her when he already felt like second fiddle."

Gisella's brow pulled in confusion. "Why have you never told me that? Rozi and I searched for those earrings for *years*."

"I thought you'd grown out of that interest.

I didn't know you were still looking for them until you came home so angry from the auction last week. At that point, it didn't seem prudent to bring up that I could have bought it ten years ago. You would have been impossible to live with."

This wasn't a play being enacted for his benefit. Gisella was genuinely taken aback and aggravated by her mother's casual attitude toward something that clearly meant a lot to her. Kaine almost felt guilty for depriving her even as he wanted to chuckle at her outrage.

"What about when the earring was actually sold to the Garrisons? *Was* it after you were born? Or—"

Her mother sighed again. "Think of the times, Gisella. Your grandmother was desperate when she married Papa. She felt disloyal for turning to another man. Of course she romanticized the story of how she and Papa got their start here, especially when relaying it to her grandchildren."

"So she lied. You've all been lying to us."

"You were a child, Gisella." Her tone suggested she still was, if this was her reaction.

"And still being treated like one, if you're keeping things from me!"

"Your grandmother is very sensitive on the topic. I've never seen the need to contradict her version with facts that serve no purpose. I should get back to my marking. Will you come by for dinner later in the week?"

"If you'd like," Gisella grumbled, planting a perfunctory kiss on her mother's cheek as Alisz offered it.

"Tell your father I said hello."

"I will," Gisella promised and they took their leave.

CHAPTER FIVE

GISELLA WAS STILL nursing impotent fury when they entered Kaine's newly renovated penthouse atop one of Manhattan's iconic skyscrapers. Like Kaine's home in San Francisco, this one was decorated in a spare, masculine style and had a view to die for.

She barely took it in, relieved to be away from her mother because she was still so mad at her, but agitated at being alone with Kaine. The click of the door as the doorman left her cases and departed made her abdomen suck in with tension.

"Let's hear it," she muttered as he poured them an aperitif.

"I told you I don't gloat."

"You still have to be reveling in being right." She wanted to knock back the lime gimlet he handed her in one gulp, but showed some restraint. Her hand shook. *What if he was also right about Benny?* She had talked tough this morning, but what would taking the fall for her cousin *really* entail?

Throughout her life, she might have had disagreements with family members, but she always trusted them to be there for her. This was the first time she felt that foundation shake beneath her. It scared the hell out of her.

"Your mother wasn't what I imagined. Given the warm way you talked about your family, I didn't picture someone as practical and incisive as she seems to be. Yet she doesn't seem to know what's going on with the mining company."

"Mother's world is a bunch of professors who talk women's studies and literature. She invests, but focuses on female entrepreneurs. She wouldn't have talked to Uncle Ben about you and Benny. Her interest in Barsi on Fifth was exhausted years ago, minding Uncle Ben and Aunt Agotha in the back of the shop while my grandparents ran the front. That's why she's such a staunch feminist. She learned exactly how demanding children are. She almost skipped motherhood altogether. She was thirty-nine when she met my father and I sometimes think she married him and had me because her sister was having kids. She felt like she was running out of time."

Gisella had only ever talked this frankly about it with Rozi. She wasn't sure why she was telling Kaine. She had barely touched her drink, but Kaine had known things about her family that even she hadn't.

Today, her mother, who was frank to a fault, had revealed a long-held lie, disillusioning her. She didn't know whom to trust or what to believe. Kaine, at least, was honest with her, if hideously blunt about it. It wasn't comfortable, but she knew where she stood.

"She was too old to have more after you? Is that why she never gave you siblings?"

"She didn't want more. Dad did. He's ten years younger than her. I remember them fighting about it. When I was eleven, he started having an affair with his secretary, Susan. She has two kids. He treats them like they're his. I guess Susan gave him the more traditional wife and family he always wanted."

A twitch around Kaine's mouth suggested he disparaged such aspirations, but he only said, "So you do have stepsiblings."

"They're a lot younger than me. I was thirteen when they married. Bitter. Susan is still very defensive. Views me as a threat, I think, since I was the reason Dad took so long to leave Mom."

She wrinkled her nose, trying not to descend into self-pity despite the fact it had been a really dark time. It still affected her. Her father doted on her in his materialistic way, but she had never quite forgiven him for his betrayal of her childish beliefs in happily-ever-after. She struggled to trust any man who professed to have feelings for her, which was a big contributor to her still-virginal state. Male promises were flimsy and men's interest in any one woman likely to wane.

"My heart broke when Dad left. Way more than Mom's. I think she was relieved. She never liked accommodating a man in her life. Maybe she even pushed him toward Susan, I don't know. The divorce was very civilized, but I was angry with Dad and I've always been closer to Mom's side of the family so I stayed with her. I only see Dad on special occasions."

"The virtues of family and love," he mused, shaking the ice in his glass before sipping.

It was another gentle yet withering indictment of the emotion she wanted to believe in, scoring surprisingly deep. Yet, given how things had played out with her mom, she had little room to argue a different view.

"I'll go change and freshen my makeup. We should leave in about an hour."

At least she had her own room. It was only a guest room, not the master, but it was still gorgeous with a small sitting area and French doors into a luxurious bathroom.

She wanted to message Rozi, but hesitated. How could she explain that she was pretending to shack up with Kaine for Benny's sake? And that a lot of what they had always believed about their grandmother was a high polish on a tarnished teapot?

She read what Rozi had sent a few hours ago. She'd been turned away from her appointment with the Rohans and was on the hunt for Viktor. She said she would report back when she had news.

Gisella set aside her phone in favor of bolstering her flagging confidence by knocking Kaine's eyes out of his sockets.

Given his seeming preference for less-is-more, she chose a very simple cranberry-red midi with a split leg. It looked quite conservative on the hanger, with a halter cut under her arms and a high collar line. The strapping in the back was more of a statement, criss-crossing her spine, but the way its jersey fabric clung to her body when she put it on was the real showstopper.

She added smoke to her eyelids, fluffed her hair and stepped into a pair of gold shoes with a chain around her ankles and a line of faux diamonds down the back of the stiletto heel.

It wasn't until she walked into the lounge,

where she found him wearing a fresh shirt and pants, nursing a drink, that she knew she hadn't dressed merely to draw his eye.

She wanted him to *want* her.

Their kiss at the auction had never left her memory. She felt like ripe fruit, about to burst from her own skin. Her braless nipples prickled and her blood was so hot, her dress ought to catch fire.

She didn't understand how being in the same room with Kaine aroused her this immediately and acutely, but it did. He did.

He didn't move, but the force of sexual attraction between them seemed to bounce back and forth, like zigzagging laces that looped and tugged, pulling them toward each other.

"I'm flattered." He smiled lazily and set aside his drink.

"I've dressed to tempt my lover. Isn't that my assignment?"

"Color me tempted."

It was nonsense banter. If they weren't at such odds, she'd call it *flirting*. Which shouldn't have the power to tighten her throat, but it did. She looked away, embarrassed by the fact she had achieved what she had hoped to and now she didn't know what to do about it.

He ambled toward her, sending her pulse skyrocketing. He touched her jaw, gently urging her to meet his gaze.

When she did, the floor seemed to disappear from beneath her. All that held her upright was his fingerprint under her chin. His expression was inscrutable, but she felt as though her virginal nerves were playing larger than a Broadway hit across her face.

Did she want to have sex with him? It would be a terrible mistake, but she wanted to anyway. It sent her heart pounding so hard, she was sure he must hear it.

"I told you my terms," he reminded quietly. Gravely. "You won't get the earring out of me. I'll still go after your cousin with every resource I have."

"Quit making presumptions about me." She gave her loose hair a haughty shake, dislodging his touch. "Even if I did want to sleep with you—which is very much an *if*. Even *if* I did, sex should be a mutual thing, not something one gives to get." As if she knew a single damned thing about it.

"It should," he agreed. "But it never is."

"Why are you so cynical?" she asked with exasperation. "Yes, sometimes people let you down. *I know that.* It doesn't mean we're all out to get you. Quit judging me by whichever woman disappointed you in the past."

He pushed his hands in his pockets. His jaw pulsed a moment as he considered her, making her nervous that she might have crossed a line. When he pivoted and moved to pick up his drink again, she blew out a subtle breath of relief.

Her lungs seized, however, when he said, "It was a little more than 'disappointment,'" he said disdainfully.

"Did you love her?" She didn't know why she asked, but the question was out before she realized it.

"I thought so."

How strange to so instantly and thoroughly

despise someone without even meeting her. Gisella concentrated on relaxing her midsection where her stomach had clenched in sick loathing, ears straining to hear him as he continued in an idle tone.

His smile was benign. "Yes, I, too, was once naive enough to think love was something I wanted. I thought a wife and kids would give me something I needed, I guess. I asked her to marry me and I suppose I should be thankful it didn't get that far, but the net result was the same. Once she had access to my office and computer, she cleaned me out. I lost the first house I'd bought along with my stock in a company I've since reacquired."

Given that he'd never had a proper home, she imagined that house must have been very important to him. She felt genuinely nauseous on his behalf and moved closer, letting him see she was appalled on his behalf.

"That's horrible! Truly." She softened her tone, beseeching him not to write her off as she added, "It doesn't mean we're all like that."

"That's the thing about foster care, though." He threw back the last of his drink. His lashes were a flinty line. "People are always taking your stuff. Even social workers make you leave a house without all your belongings. I try not to care about material things anymore, but living comfortably is important to me. And it still makes me furious if someone takes what I've worked hard to acquire."

That's why he was feeling so murderous toward Benny. And why he looked at her dressing to kill as a false promise. A ploy.

How could she convince him that people could be generous and trustworthy? That desire and passion—*her* desire for *him*—was real?

A buzz sounded, startling her out of taking a step she might not be able to come back from.

"The car is here." He shrugged on his jacket and opened the door.

The word *Wait* stayed lodge in her throat as she left with him.

* * *

Kaine knew from his report on Gisella's family that her father owned one of the most highly regarded ad agencies on Madison Avenue. He had pulled out all the stops for his wife's birthday, filling the Waldorf Astoria's Starlight Ballroom with a fountain of Dom Pérignon and swag bags stuffed with the luxury brands he represented.

He greeted Gisella with a warm smile and shook Kaine's hand as she introduced him. "I'm, um, staying with Kaine while he's in New York."

Her father did a small double take. "That sounds serious."

"Dad." Gisella cut him off with a smile that looked more like gritted teeth. "We'll find a drink and let you continue greeting your guests." She drew Kaine into the heart of the party.

"Your mother said we sounded serious, too," Kaine recalled as they moved to the bar. "Should I brace for a shotgun in my armpit?"

"No. It's just—it doesn't matter."

He thought she might be blushing again, but the bartender asked them for their order. He watched her as he waited for their drinks.

She'd been quiet on the way over, perhaps rethinking her strategy, now she was armed with the knowledge he was capable of being a fool.

He wasn't sure what had made him share one of his few personal details that wasn't as easily found online. While she'd been changing, he'd been brooding on what she'd told him of her family. She'd seemed legitimately angry with her mother for keeping secrets and embarrassed that she had believed an untruth for so long.

She had accused him of gloating, but he'd been too busy trying to figure out how she was making him think they had something in common. He had no family and she was so rich with it, she could afford to see her father only on special occasions. Yet somehow she portrayed herself as being set apart from all of them. Her mother was career focused, her father had built the family he'd preferred with someone else's children.

Deep down, she was the same as him. Alone.

He knew how to overcome that, he'd been thinking, when she had strolled into his ruminations wearing a siren's dress. He had wanted to say, *Come with me and neither of us will ever be alone again.*

He wanted her in ways that went beyond peeling away that dress and pressing his lips to her skin—although he craved *that* like air. But he wanted inside her head. He wanted to know if the things she said were coming from her heart. Did she even have one?

It doesn't mean we're all like that.

He wasn't a man who feared risk, but he didn't take stupid ones. Given her cousin's treachery, he couldn't afford to trust her.

But he wanted to.

And that made her more dangerous than any woman he'd ever met.

"You really don't care for parties," Kaine said as he drew her onto the dance floor. "You're tense."

He was playing his fingertips over the laces at the back of her dress as though strumming a stringed instrument. She couldn't help but flex in reaction.

"I'm feeling very much on display. Are we accomplishing what you hoped?"

She kept thinking that if she could show him good faith as far as their deal went, he might begin to see her differently.

"You're very beautiful. Of course you draw attention."

She glanced up at him, ready to dismiss the compliment as a platitude, but she caught him staring down another man who may or may not have been checking out her butt.

She bit the corner of her mouth. Possessiveness wasn't sexy, she reminded herself.

But she was succumbing to it herself, taking every chance to stake a claim by setting her hand on his arm or brushing one of her stray hairs from his jacket.

He was ridiculously handsome, standing taller than most of the men here, hair in rumpled bed-head spikes. His suit was more beautifully tailored than anyone's, but he wasn't nearly as buttoned down as the rest of this crowd and all the sexier for his less civilized demeanor.

He was a well-fed wolf among groomed show dogs, ten times as dangerous and able to take control of the pack merely by walking among them.

He seduced her by existing.

"As PR campaigns go, this is a start," he answered, reminding her this wasn't a date. It was an exercise in reparation.

She'd seen a few expressions shift as she'd introduced him. People were trying to place his name and connecting him in their heads to the Barsi reputation.

"It will be more effective once the gossip has a chance to percolate." He drifted his hand upward to catch a loose tendril of her hair, tugging just hard enough she tilted her head back in response. "Perhaps we should give them something to talk about."

She almost turned her heel and tightened her hand on his shoulder to steady herself. "If you want to kiss me, ask. Don't turn it into something I have to do to uphold my side of this bargain."

She half expected another cynical remark about how little he trusted her. Instead, his gaze warmed.

"I have a deadly fascination with this fiery side of you. I'm like a kid playing with matches." He twirled her hair around his finger, drawing her head back another inch, trapping her like that. "I want to kiss you." His expression tightened. "I'm dying to know if that passion you showed me the first time is still there. If it's real."

She couldn't dance when she was trying to hold herself together. Conflict and longing engulfed her. She might have fought it, but behind his stony look, she caught a flash, quick as a glint in a mirror, that made her think she read the same emotions in him.

She slid her hand from his shoulder to the back of his neck, exerting pressure.

He accepted the invitation with the unerring swoop of a raptor.

And she was carried away.

Like him, she had wanted to know. Now she did. They were exactly as cataclysmic as they'd been that first time. *More.* This time she was primed by knowing him a little better. Primed by nearly two weeks of wondering if it could have possibly been this good and it *was*.

His mouth scraped across hers, wild and raw. Incendiary. His hands hardened on her back, ironing her to his front. Lights sparkled behind her eyes.

She basked in the carnal roughness. It spoke of greed and need and a desire that couldn't be quenched. Not until they could strip naked and the hard shape imprinting against her abdomen was soothing and inciting the molten ache in her center. Her need was so acute, she felt it as a sob in her throat.

Actual pain pulled at her scalp, snapping her back to reality as he held her still, refusing to let her follow his mouth when he lifted his head. Her lips burned and her breath soughed across her parted lips.

"Oh, *God*," she gasped, horrified with herself. "My father probably saw that."

"It was just a kiss," he murmured, arms sheltering her now.

His words hurt, though. That had been a lot more than a kiss to her, but as she blinked open her eyes, she realized he had somehow shifted them into a corner where a stolen moment wasn't so scandalous. His wide shoulders shielded her from prying eyes, giving her a chance to collect herself.

"That's all anyone will have seen, anyway," he added, lips grazing the tip of her ear through the fall of her hair. "I can feel your heart racing." His hand was moving in a soothing circle across the laces of her dress.

Beneath the fist she'd curled into his lapel, she felt the answering slam of his own heart. It was as surprising as it was elating.

"What now, pussycat?" His voice sounded almost as drugged as she felt his breath against her hair make her scalp prickle.

She kept her nose against the silk of his tie, willing her trembles to subside, but they only increased as she realized what he was asking. Stay or go?

Go where? How far? How fast?

The music changed and she heard a voice nearby.

She couldn't stay here and act like her world hadn't been turned inside out. She swallowed and said, "We should leave."

Moments later, they had said their goodbyes and were in the back of his car.

The night air seemed thick, creating a bubble of pressure around them as they made the short drive in the dark. Her mouth was dry, her limbs not hers. As they walked into his building and rode the elevator upward, she had to remind herself to breathe. It wasn't until he was closing the door with a definitive click that he openly acknowledged why they had hurried back here.

"Everything I've said remains the same." He stayed by the door, sexual energy radiating off him in lethal waves. "If that's not what you want, we'll retire to our separate rooms."

Her throat grew thick with a lump of hurt

and her eyes stung. "Is it so hard for you to believe I'm experiencing genuine animal attraction?"

It was more than that. As much as she found him physically enthralling, she was drawn to the man behind the facade of laid-back control. He already had the power to hurt her, but also the power to make her laugh and hope for things she knew were ridiculous, but she hoped anyway.

"I'm quite sure animal attraction is what we're both experiencing." His words, the smoky tone in his voice, electrified her. "But I'm not going to let you use it against me."

"I'm not trying to," she insisted. She heard the white lie within her own words, though. She did want something from him. Trust. She wanted him to believe her. Some corner of her brain thought that if she slept with him, and demanded nothing afterward, she would prove to him that she wasn't like the rest.

She usually had a better grasp on reality. On her own motives, but she wanted to sleep with him. That was the glaring, shocking, painful truth. She could wait until tomorrow or the next day or the next, but she would still feel this yearning. This desire to be closer. To open herself up and understand him. She didn't want to risk waiting until Benny reappeared. Everything would be different then. Maybe worse, maybe better. She didn't know, but it would be different.

In this moment, they were equals of a sort. She was neither innocent nor guilty. He was neither victim nor villain. They were two people with one thing between them—desire.

"I don't want anything else in the world right now except to feel your hands on me," she admitted baldly.

He dragged in a ragged breath like he'd been sucker punched. He pushed off the door to come toward her.

The flutters in her belly became a wobble that went all the way into her knees.

"You're sure?" He used light fingers to brush her hair behind her shoulder, not even touching her skin, but causing her to hold very still, paralyzed by anticipation. "Because

I want to put my mouth on you. I want to claim every inch of you with every inch of me."

"Yes," she breathed. "That." Whatever was in her hands fell to the floor in a pair of muted thumps.

He lowered his head to set a damp, open-mouthed kiss on the point of her bare shoulder. The action raised her nipples so they stung while her whole body seemed to rise and reach toward him the way a flower stretched from the earth to seek the sun.

His firm hands encircled her waist and he buried his mouth against her neck, taking erotic mock bites up her nape so she shivered and grasped at his arms to steady herself, then turned her own mouth into his neck to taste his salty skin.

"I'll get lipstick on your collar," she warned as she tried to nuzzle past it.

"Good." He bit her earlobe, making her scalp tingle. A rush of damp heat flowed into her loins. "Mark me however you like." His tongue flicked into the sensitive hollow beneath her ear.

She wanted to laugh with mad triumph at the thought. It was insane to feel this possessive, but she did. She wanted the world to know he was hers. She wanted *him* to know it and took hold of his tie, holding him still while she sucked the side of his neck, branding him, then licking to soothe the sting.

His teeth flashed before he covered her mouth in a kiss that slammed through her, topping her act of claiming with his own— not by being aggressive, but with the sheer power of response he pulled from her as he tenderly savaged her mouth.

He lifted his head and looked down her front, a barbarian surveying the bounty he'd captured.

This is it, she thought distantly. She would lose her virginity to him, but she felt no hesitation or regret. This was what she had always longed for, a man whose touch swept her away. An encounter that was so encompassing, she couldn't stop herself. It was madness, yes, but thrilling and real. Pure excitement and nothing held back.

She moved on instinct to cup the back of his neck and urge him to cover her offered mouth with his own.

The world fell away in a fresh masculine growl and the erotic sweep of his tongue. Hard arms closed around her, crushing her breath from her body as she mashed her aching breasts against the hard plate of his chest.

His hands roamed hungrily across her back, one tangling in the strings at her back, the other moving the silky fabric against her buttocks so the hem tickled the backs of her thighs. She wriggled in response, feeling her skirt climb against her hips so the front of her thighs met the abrasion of his trousers. She pulled back to tug open the buttons of his shirt and brought her hands down to claim the hot muscles and silky hair she revealed.

He was fascinating. Gorgeous and hot and hard. Animalistic and responsive, pecs twitching under her touch, utterly compelling. She knew nothing more in those seconds than the feel of him under her palms. She bathed his skin with her humid breath, heard him hiss as she chased her mouth across to his tight nipple, then sought out the other one.

He gathered her hair away from her neck and dragged at it to expose her throat to his hot mouth, then gently bit the corded muscle, sending a shudder of weakness down her spine. She arched her whole body in surrender, mashing her mound into the firm ridge behind his fly.

Wild, wild, wild. Now his teeth scraped across the fabric where her braless nipples stood at attention, making her whimper at the muted threat of pain, but the sensation wasn't nearly acute enough to assuage the ache.

He dropped to his knees, making her stagger slightly as her hands dropped to her sides, no longer holding on to him.

He looked up at her as his hands climbed her thighs, taking her dress up, watching for her reaction, ensuring this was what she wanted.

It was. Her loins were pulsing in anticipation, her stomach fluttering, all of her so hot she could hardly draw air. She nearly fell into the molten gold of his eyes and would happily incinerate there.

When her scrap of a thong was revealed, he lowered his gaze to the veil of whisper-thin silk. She'd chosen the burgundy lace for his pleasure. It had been a conscious decision, but not something she had fully acknowledged to herself at the time.

He licked his lips and her inner muscles clenched with anticipation. Heat flooded into her loins and her pulse seemed to originate there, throbbing as he traced a single fingertip across the top of her thong, from hip to hip, barely grazing her mound.

She sobbed, paralyzed by expectation, waiting and yearning and *needing* more.

His finger went under the narrow band at her hip and tugged.

Her breath caught and the ache between her thighs intensified. She shifted slightly, making it easier for him to ease them down.

She was panting, thinking she ought to feel self-conscious, but she was thinking only how utterly in thrall she was. Whatever level of arousal she might have felt in the past was magnified a thousand times. Need gripped her. Need to hurry, but stand still. To throw herself at him, but be whatever he wanted her to be. She was with him in this moment and letting it unfold however he wanted to make it happen.

The silk fell to her ankles and he eased one foot out, his hand scalding on her calf. He lowered his head to kiss the inside of her knee.

She staggered and reached for his shoulders.

"Lean on the sofa." His voice was whiskey and velvet, leather and command.

She had lost all sense of her place in the universe and was surprised to find the sofa right behind her. Her hips met the firmness of it and she balanced against it. She scrambled her hands against the leather to steady herself, fingernails stabbing against the hide as he took his time stropping his cheek against her inner thigh.

"So soft," he murmured.

She was going to die. Die of waiting and wanting. Her blood was molasses, her eyes damp and stinging as she closed them. She bit her lip, waiting and waiting and then…

A hot, wet stroke strummed exquisite sensations all the way through her.

A gasp of delight escaped her.

He set her foot on the floor, shoes spaced wide to accommodate his kneeling between her legs. She was trapped in a delicious vise then, skirt up, exposed to him and pinned between the sofa and his tender exploration. Her fingernails were likely to puncture the leather she was in such a state of agony as she stood and endured his skillful, wicked insistence on driving her utterly mad.

He took his time, seeming to take as much pleasure as she did from each caress, drawing her to a state of acute excitement, then slowing, soothing, until she was breathing jaggedly and nearly begging before he incited her toward the edge again.

Her legs were shaking beneath the restless caress of his hands. She began rising into the rhythm of his ministrations, saying his name in ragged whispers, mindless with pleasure. She couldn't take it anymore.

"I'm ready," she gasped, spearing her hand into his hair. "Take off your clothes. I want to feel you. *Do it.*"

He stayed exactly where he was. He circled one arm around her hips and moved his other hand to the top of her thigh. His thumb caressed where his tongue was already making her crazy, then gently probed and laved and stole what remained of her control.

She couldn't withstand the intensity, the pleasure, couldn't hold back her release. He drove her to climax and it struck like a train, crashing through her as a glittering cataclysm that rocked her with waves of pleasure, making her cry out in joyful abandon, utterly at his mercy, on her feet only because he held her there.

She didn't even know who she was after that, except a pure being shimmering in the aftermath of orgasm. She was dimly aware that his deep caresses eased and the firm arm around her hips relaxed. He rose before her, sweeping her dress over her head as he went.

She let her arms fall as he discarded the dress. She stood naked before him, wearing only her heels, still reeling. He skimmed his gaze down her trembling form, point to point, breast tips and navel, damp curls and weak knees and wicked gilded shoes.

"Do I need a condom?"

Did he ever. She nodded dumbly.

"Bedroom, then."

"I can't walk," she admitted in a whisper.

He stooped and swung her up, clutching her high against his chest as he carried her like a virgin sacrifice into his room.

CHAPTER SIX

KAINE SET HER on the bed and yanked at his shirt.

She wanted to watch him, but she wanted to unbuckle her shoes. She sat up, but her hands trembled, making her clumsy.

"You can leave them on," he said in a growl, but she was already dropping the first one to the floor.

She looked up as she worked on the second. His eyes were bright gold, his cheeks flushed, his mouth pulled against his teeth in a hunter's feral grin. She managed to get the other shoe unbuckled and he swept it off her foot.

"This," he said with avid hunger, cupping her face and kissing her so she melted onto her back and he followed her down. His naked chest brushed against hers, making her squirm and stroke as much of that glorious skin of his as she could reach.

He lifted onto his elbow and looked her over again, sweeping a hand from her shoulder down her side into her waist, smoothed over her hip and down her thigh. "This is what I've been waiting for." He returned to squeeze her thigh.

"Me, too," she confessed.

His hand traveled farther, came up to cup her breast and he leaned to take her nipple into his mouth, not gentle, but she liked his greed. She stroked her hands through his hair, loving that she was pushing him to the limits of his restraint. And his sucking flooded her with fresh arousal. When he roamed his hand down her abdomen and caressed between her thighs, he groaned with pleasure at finding her slick and ready. She lifted wantonly into his caress, inviting everything he desired.

When he rose to stand over her, she was ready to weep with loss, but eager for the next step. He toed off his own shoes and stripped his lower half in a sweep, taking everything at once and throwing his final sock onto the pile as he straightened.

He was beyond ready for her, hard and thick and flushed. He took himself in hand and squeezed as though trying to hold back his release. She swallowed, suddenly apprehensive.

"What's wrong?" He was watching her.

"Nothing," she assured him. This was just very real all of a sudden.

He drew a condom from the night table and applied it, then joined her on the bed. Kissed her and pushed his knee between hers to part her legs.

The heel of her hand went to his shoulder of its own accord, not quite pushing him away, but signaling hesitation.

He drew back and the passion in his face altered, hardened with suspicion. "What do you want?"

He looked...ferocious. Brutal, but not in a way that threatened to hurt her. More like a brutally clinical and sudden *absence* of passion. The fire of desire was still there behind his eyes, but it was banked. He would weigh the strength of it against whatever she named as her condition for continuing to participate.

Her chest grew tight. That wasn't what was going on *at all*. In fact, the only thing she wanted in this moment was to overcome her own nerves.

"It's okay. I want to. I do." She drew him to kiss her, needing the mindlessness of passion to sweep her through the awkwardness of her first time.

He hesitated, then returned her kiss. Took it over to kiss her more deeply. And he touched her again, sawing his hand sweetly between her thighs, until her own hands didn't so much move over his neck and back and chest as drag at him, trying to absorb him. She paused a few times to dig her nails into his back when a particular sensation nearly sent her over the crest, but he seemed to know when she was getting close and eased back so she was tracing restless patterns again.

He was making her crazy and the way he sucked on her tongue was positively carnal.

She thought she would die if he didn't let her climax soon.

"Now?" His face was a mask of intensity, all of him hard as iron with only a shred of civility left in his atavistic gaze.

"Yes," she sobbed, parting her thighs in welcome.

His shoulders shook as he moved atop her and guided himself into place. Her center was so hot and needy she welcomed the pressure and the thick intrusion that stretched—

She gasped at the smarting sting and tensed beneath him. Her knees locked themselves against his hips, urging him to stillness.

He lifted his head, concern breaking through the carnal lust fogging his eyes.

"Hurt?" he asked, gruff and confused. "I thought…" He started to withdraw, but she tightened her hold to keep him where he was.

"It's okay. It's normal. Keep going. It feels really good." So good. She arched on instinct, took him deeper.

It seemed to be his undoing. His gaze clouded again. His nostrils flared. He cupped her head and watched her, teeth clenched, taking it slow, making sure she was receiving pleasure, but letting all his weight sink onto her before he lifted and did it again.

She thrilled at the way he forged into her. Filled her. Made her utterly his while she took him and held him and owned him.

She closed her eyes and bit her lip and gasped at a rush of sensation so intense it was agonizing. Her hands slid to his buttocks, exploring their flexing shape as they both trembled.

He withdrew and thrust faster. Deeper. And deeper still.

Everything about the moment impacted. The way they fit, the friction of skin on skin, belly to belly, the feel of his hair roughened thighs against her smooth ones, the tension across his shoulders, the suck of his lips against her neck. He shifted, fingers finding her nipple and making her toes curl.

The ragged edge of his breath matched hers. Moans emanated from her throat without conscious thought. She stroked from the silk of his hair down the damp hollow of his spine and traced the line between his buttocks.

As if it was a signal, he began to thrust in earnest. It was incredible. She lost herself to the magnificence of thorough lovemaking.

This had been worth waiting for. *He* had. As her tension grew, she hugged him tight with everything in her, all of her so hot, she was scorching, but she reveled in the inferno. The intensity became nearly more than she could bear. The prick of her nails turned to scrapes as she tried to bring him deeper. Harder. *More.*

Her body arched beneath his, meeting his thrusts and clinging as he left. She turned her mouth against his shoulder and her teeth bit down, fighting the culmination because she wanted this to go on forever, but needed release so badly.

"Let go. Let me feel it," he ground out. "Now."

She couldn't have held back one millisecond longer. The wave of orgasm swept her up and crashed through her, catching her in a paroxysm that wrenched exquisitely, even as it held her on that plain of abject pleasure, pulling him in with her at the same time.

He ground himself hard against her, hips firm to hers, his climax tearing a shout of triumph from him. He pulsed within her while the rest of him shuddered and their combined rippling waves of pleasure held her in thrall. She had never felt closer to another person in her life.

As the fog of lust receded, Kaine became aware that Gisella was panting beneath him. Trembles were still working their way through her. He had an urge to tuck her close and soothe her.

The strength of his own climax had nearly killed him. It must have scared the hell out of her.

Seeing as she'd been a virgin.

Really? That was why she'd been sending mixed messages?

He'd been stunned when she'd flinched as he had thrust into her with confidence, certain she was more than ready for him. He had never hurt a woman in his life, not physically and definitely not in such an intimate way. It hadn't occurred to him she might be new to this, not the way she was responding to him.

It's normal, she had said, and he'd realized what she meant.

He would have withdrawn at that point, but he'd been aroused beyond rational thought. She had practically begged him to finish the job, and the uncomfortable truth was, he might have resorted to pleading if she hadn't. He might have given her anything she demanded—which is what he had thought she was planning when she had had that moment of apprehension.

She'd wanted to continue, though, and aside from ensuring she was with him every step of the way, he hadn't thought of a damned thing except how good she felt. He'd been immersed in a kind of ecstasy he hadn't known was possible. It was all the sweeter because, for those timeless moments, he had believed the only trade-off was that they were two people who were perfectly matched, giving each other exactly what they were getting—sexual gratification.

Coming down off that, however, his ingrained suspicions returned.

Why had she given him her virginity? There was no way she would give that up freely to a man she barely knew. Not without trying to obligate him after the fact.

He didn't know which was more acute—his disappointment in her, for her trickery, or his disgust with himself, for letting down his guard and allowing it to happen. He was such a *chump*.

He withdrew as gently as he could, noting a stain of red on the condom. He rolled for a tissue and discarded it in the waste bin off that side of the bed. Then he stayed on his back and stared at the ceiling.

"What do you want, Gisella?" His tone was rough, his throat still raw from his shout of conquest when he'd lost himself in culmination. It had been worth nearly anything except this pall of self-contempt.

He turned his head in time to catch her flinch. She blinked her eyes open to reveal shadows of hurt dimming her dreamy meadow-green irises. "What do you mean?"

"You were a virgin."

"Is that an accusation?" She dropped her hand off the side of the bed and dragged at the bedspread until she'd drawn the edge across her middle. "We all start out that way, in case you weren't aware. So what?"

He snorted. "You're giving yours away to *me*? For *free*?"

"Is that so hard to believe?"

"It's impossible to believe. What are you planning to ask me for? The earring?"

"No! Nothing."

"Right," he disparaged tiredly. "You wanted to put me in a position of feeling obliged. But I don't feel duty-bound to offer you the earring or leniency toward your cousin—"

"Shut *up*." She tried to sit up, but the fold in the blanket and the fact he was lying on the other side of it hindered her. She settled for bracing on an elbow beside him, quilted bedspread twisted across her hips and hugged to her breasts. "This has nothing to do with Benny or the earring. I wanted to m—" She glared at him as though he was the one doing something wrong.

"Marry me?" he guessed with abject disbelief.

"Make love," she corrected, gaze dropping while her brows remained tortured with self-consciousness.

The phrase cut through him like a scythe. "Either way, that's not where we're going. I lost my shirt to a woman once. It's never going to happen again."

"Did I ask you for marriage and a baby carriage? *No.* But is a shred of warmth too much to ask? You know what I want? To get out of this bed without further humiliation! Turn around."

"Don't be shy on my account. I'm intimately acquainted."

She threw off the blanket and rose to stand over the bed like a Valkyrie, hair practically crackling. "You know what I wanted when we came in here? A nice experience. I thought we were giving each other pleasure. You don't have to say you love me, but you could act like you *like* me. You could say you *enjoyed* it. I don't think that's too much to ask for my first time. Thanks for ruining it by being a suspicious jerk."

She started for the door.

"Gisella," he ground out, not even sure why he was calling her back. Maybe because he'd seen that disillusioned look on a face once before, in a mirror, after he'd realized how badly he had misplaced his own trust. It sickened him to be on the receiving end of it.

"Go to hell." She walked out.

CHAPTER SEVEN

KAINE PRIDED HIMSELF on being a generous lover. Perhaps it was motivated by a desire to stay ahead and not owe his partner anything, especially satisfaction, but he had been on the wrong side of charity and, worse, selfishness. If he liked to have the upper hand and use it to keep a firm grasp of power, it was because he never again wanted to feel power*less*.

But he felt utterly helpless as she exited. He'd let his ingrained distrust turn her first time into a disappointment. He might not be a romantic, but even his cynical soul believed such a thing ought to be a little bit special. Maybe not perfect. His had been awkward as hell, but he looked back on his sexual initiation with sheepish fondness, not bitter disappointment. It galled him even more that he'd tarnished what had been a singular experience for him.

He couldn't leave things like this. He stood and yanked on his pants, following as far as the lounge. In her bedroom, he heard drawers slamming. Packing, most likely, mere hours after she had unpacked in there.

A jagged sensation in his chest tore at his heart. How would he get her to stay? Threaten her family again? Somehow, in trying to maintain the upper hand, he was left feeling as though he'd crawled out of the sewer. With his lungs aching, he searched his blank mind for some way to come back from his behavior. To make up with her.

Into the silence, her phone rang. She had dropped it on the floor between the sofa and the door. Her dress and underwear were discarded next to it, reminding him starkly of how perfectly they'd been attuned to one another less than an hour ago.

The phone read "Unknown" but the sequence of numbers was obviously intercontinental. He picked it up on reflex and slid to answer. "Hello?"

A woman's voice choked, "Oh, God. I dialed the wrong number. I'm so sorry."

"Wait. Are you looking for Gisella? Is this Rozi?"

"Yes," she said in a distressed whimper. "Who's this?"

"I'll get her."

She hated him. *Hated* him. Mean, small, *awful* man.

With shaking hands, she pulled on her robe, then packed. What would he do if she left? Go after her family? Accuse her of trying to trade her virginity for her freedom from this fake, dead-end facade of a relationship?

Hopelessness overwhelmed her and the tears she'd been fighting burned hotter, blurring her vision.

How had she gotten so tangled up with such a cynical bastard? She wasn't one of those foolish women who thought they could change a man. She knew she couldn't find his heart and make it grow three sizes. He had promised her nothing and delivered nothing. Why was she so devastated?

Because she had crawled into his bed offering more than her virginity. She had been willing to offer her heart. Damned near everything within her, if she was honest, and he had rebuffed all of it. Her whole being felt turned inside out.

She moved into the bathroom to wash off her makeup, then continued splashing the cool water on her face, trying to dilute the salty shame burning her eyelids.

"Gisella." He knocked and entered wearing only his pants.

She said something she said only to men who tried to grope her on the subway.

He didn't flinch, only held out her phone. "It's your cousin. It was ringing when I went into the lounge."

"Which one?" She straightened and swiped a hand towel across her face, then took the phone. "Hello?"

"It's me," Rozi said in a choked voice. She was crying. "I've been arrested."

"What?" Gisella felt the impact of the edge of the sink against her hip as she slumped against it in shock. *"For what?"*

"They think I stole Viktor's earring."

"Oh, my God." Their promise to do whatever it took to get the earrings came back to Gisella, making her spit out a disbelieving, "You didn't, did you?"

"Of course not!" Rozi was trying to catch her breath between her fear-laced sobs. "I w-w-was there last night and this morning it was g-g-gone. But it w-w-wasn't me. I need a law-lawyer. Can you—?"

"Of course. Yes. Calm down. Let me get a pen and paper. I'll look after everything." Her heart pounded as she hurried past Kaine into the bedroom.

He had to be able to hear Rozi as clearly as she could. She didn't look at him, not wanting to see his contemptuous expression indicting her cousin as a thief in jail where he no doubt believed they all belonged.

He left the bedroom as she dumped her purse and scrabbled for a pen, but surprised her by meeting her in the lounge with a pad of paper.

She knelt at the coffee table, saying, "Is there a policeman I can talk to? I need him to tell me how this works."

Her grandmother had insisted they all speak Hungarian growing up. There was no language barrier as Gisella was efficiently schooled on the steps she needed to follow to have her cousin released. When he put her back on with Rozi, Gisella did her best to re-assure her near-hysterical cousin.

"I'm going to make some calls and send a lawyer to bail you out. Then I'll book a flight," she promised. "I'll be there as soon as I can."

"We can leave in four hours," Kaine said above her. He was holding his own phone and took a photo of the notes she'd made.

"What?" She'd lost track of him in the time she'd been talking to the police.

"The flight is ten hours. Tell her you should be there before she has to spend the night."

Rather than argue with him, she repeated it to Rozi. Anything to calm her.

"Can you tell Mom and Dad?" Rozi choked. "I only get one call."

"Of course. I'm going to take care of all of this," Gisella promised, even though she had never once bailed a person out of jail, especially in a foreign country. Once the family banded together, however, mountains could be moved.

"They're telling me to wrap up. I'm so sorry, Gizi. Uncle Ben didn't answer and—"

"Don't apologize. I love you. I'll do anything for you. You know that. I'll see you soon. I promise." She hung up and shakily called her mother.

"Alisz Barsi," she answered in a sleepy voice.

"Sorry to wake you, Mom, but Aunt Agotha will need you." Gisella rose to pace restlessly, explaining about Rozi. "I'm going to look up some lawyer numbers in Budapest—"

"My lawyer is already making calls," Kaine said, following to stand in the doorway of her bedroom, once again causing her to stare at him dumbly. "He should have someone at the station within a few hours."

Her mother said something and Gisella dragged her attention back to the call, paraphrasing what Kaine had said.

"No, I don't know how much," she replied to her mother's question. "But I'll let you know where to wire it as soon as I do. Tell Aunty I'm flying over and she shouldn't worry." As if. Rozi's mother had received all the emotions that Gisella's mother hadn't. She would be hysterical, which was why Rozi had tried their uncle first, then Gisella. She probably would have tried Gisella's mother next, rather than her own.

Gisella ended the call and set the phone on the dresser top. She was shaking. The seriousness was beginning to impact her, but she pushed it to the edges of her consciousness.

"For all my mother's faults, she's a rock in a crisis," she remarked, maybe just to reassure herself. She always tried to emulate her mother in that regard. She looked into the drawer of clothes, but couldn't remember what she was doing.

Kaine picked up an accent throw off the foot of the bed and came to wrap it around her shoulders. "You're in shock. Sit down before you fall down." He tried to ease her toward the bed.

"I can't." She tried to brush the blanket off. "I'll fall apart. I need to pack."

He firmed his hold around her. "It's the middle of the night and there's nothing we can do for the next four hours. Sit for a minute." He dragged her into his lap as he lowered to the edge of the bed. His strong arms gathered her in, warm and reassuring.

She resisted, mind still in Budapest, where her cousin was being led back to a cell. "I have to *do* something. Rozi needs me."

"Shh, it's okay." He settled her closer.

"No, it's not! She's in *jail.*" She clenched her eyes tight, but a tear squeezed out. "I'm really scared for her. She wouldn't steal. Whatever you think of me—"

"Shh, listen. This is important," he said against her hair, arms like iron, forcing her to stay exactly where she was. "She'll be okay." He sounded so sure, she couldn't help taking heart. "You said she's resilient? That people underestimate her? That's good. It's the ones who go in acting like they have something to prove that get into trouble. You, I would worry about. You don't know when to back down, but she grew up with siblings, didn't she? Is she the oldest?"

She had a feeling he was making her talk for the sake of it. To distract her. "Middle. One older brother, and a younger brother and sister."

"I bet she's one of the great mediators of the world."

"She is." Any family disagreement, especially among the cousins, had Rozi stepping up first to smooth it over.

Gisella clenched her fist where it sat against

his chest, sniffing because he was being really, really nice right now. Why?

"Tell me more about her," he said in that soothing voice.

"She's sensitive. Intuitive. Kind." Her composure was beginning to crack under the pressures seemingly coming from all sides. "She's my best friend. I'd do anything for her. We always thought we'd go to Hungary together, but I wanted to see *you* again." She felt so guilty about that now. She hung her head against his chest. "And we made this stupid promise to each other years ago, after my parents divorced. We swore we wouldn't have sex until we were in love, and I was in bed with you while she was being *arrested*—"

"Shh." His hands smoothed across her back, drawing her in as she broke down and began to cry in earnest.

Her tears weren't all for her cousin, though. They were for the mess she was in with him. The lovemaking and the arguing and the hurt he'd delivered by acting so mistrustful, then taking care of things so swiftly in her time of crisis. It was horribly confusing to hate him and feel grateful at the same time.

"Why are you being so nice?"

He drew a breath, but his chest stayed expanded and firm under her wet cheek, prolonging the silence.

"Because of earlier? Damn you, Kaine!" She knocked her fist against his chest. "You don't owe me anything."

His breath eased out in a pained sigh that hurt her all the more.

She would have dragged herself off his lap, but he held her and rocked her.

"Be calm, Gisella," he insisted, making crooning noises until she lay limp with exhaustion in his arms. He petted her hair and soothed her back and she started to relax into sleep, then jerked awake with a gasp of alarm.

"It's okay," he murmured, his voice more rumble beneath her ear than a voice she heard externally. "I'll wake you when it's time to go. But get some rest or you'll be no use to her."

"I can't," she wailed softly, but sleep dragged at her. The last few days had been far too much to cope with. She was emotionally drained, physically exhausted and her mind wanted to escape from all of it. She slipped into sleep cradled in his arms.

You don't owe me anything.

That's not what this was, but he didn't want to explain that his desire to help didn't spring from a sense of obligation after taking her virginity. It wasn't even reparation for what had come after, although that was part of it.

He had watched her go pale at Rozi's call and hadn't been able to stand the anxiety that gripped her. He would do anything to assuage it.

Which might make him a softheaded fool. Again. But she was in his arms again and he closed his eyes to savor the feel of her.

His phone vibrated in his shirt pocket. He shifted slightly to see the face. His lawyer's name showed up on the screen.

Reluctantly, he settled her onto the bed,

tucked a blanket across her and moved out of the room to take the call where his voice wouldn't disturb her.

Gisella was deeply asleep in a hammock, swaying and swaying. The hammock was starting to tip—

She threw out a hand to catch herself, flashing her eyes open. Her fingers landed on Kaine's thigh where he sat beside her on the bed. His palm was stroking her arm rhythmically as he gently eased her awake.

Had they—? Oh, God, they had. She recalled their intimacy in a rush of appalled memory. And afterward he had thought she'd made love with him only to barter her virginity. Then Rozi had called and—

"Oh, *God*." She sat up and her brain seemed to fly forward to smack the inside of her forehead, causing an instant headache. She touched her brow. "What time is it?"

"It's okay." He stayed sitting next to her. "We have to leave in about thirty minutes.

You should dress and check what I've packed for you."

"Did you sleep?" His stubble had darkened. His eyes were bruised and weary. The clock read 4:22 a.m.

"I wanted to be available if my lawyer called again. He has a woman headed to the detention facility now. She'll see Rozi, offer representation. I've emailed you her contact details if you want to forward it to your mom and the rest of your family, so they know things are progressing."

She sagged a little, wondering how she would have accomplished so much if left to her own devices.

"I can't thank you enough for fast-tracking things." She couldn't look at him. Her face grew so hot and tight it hurt. "Please bill me for all the expenses. Between me and the rest of my family—"

"Gisella—"

"I won't accept that I've already paid for this, Kaine." She scooted off the far side of the bed. "I couldn't bear it."

"That's not what this is," he said, quiet and implacable, tone so dark it made her stomach wobble.

"I'll settle up once Rozi is out and I can think properly," she swore, gathering up her clothes to take them into the bathroom, where she dressed and brushed her teeth.

She felt guilty for falling asleep, but was marginally less emotional after a few hours of rest. She was clearheaded enough to finish packing and catch up with the messages on her phone. She forwarded Kaine's lawyer's info to her mother and noted the contact details for friends of the family her mother urged her to use in Budapest if she needed anything while she was there.

As she was thanking her mother, Rozi rang through with a face call.

"I'm leaving for the airport right now," Gisella told her the second it connected.

Rozi looked pale and tense, but not as distressed as she had sounded before. She appeared to be in the back of a town car. "I was hoping to catch you before you left. I'm out. It's okay. You don't have to come."

"You're on your way to the airport? Coming home?" Gisella's tension deflated, leaving her so weak she had to sit down on the bed to keep from collapsing onto the floor.

"I have to stay in Hungary a little longer. The lawyer thinks it will all be dismissed very quickly, though."

Gisella looked to where Kaine had come to stand in the doorway of her bedroom. She could reimburse him, but how would she ever really repay him for getting a lawyer there? One who had acted so quickly and efficiently?

She flicked her hot gaze back to Rozi, emotion tightening her throat so her voice was raspy. "I'll still come and stay with you while you wait it out."

"You don't have to. There's nothing you can do and I'm—" Her cousin looked to her right, profile flexing with uncertainty. "I have to stay with Viktor. He, um, found the earring and paid my bail, which is how I got out. I'm his responsibility until your lawyer gets the rest of it sorted. Thank you *so much* for her. I'll pay you back. I promise. But she said I should stick around because I might have to appear before a judge. She'll try to make that happen as quickly as possible. I know you want more details, but can we talk later? I have to call Mom. She's left a million messages. I'll call back when things have settled down, okay?"

"Yes, of course, but Rozi—forget the earring, okay? It's not worth this kind of trouble."

"I know." Rozi gave her a look of angst. "In fact, will you talk to Grandmamma about it? Because I don't think we have the full story there. Oh, there's Mom, trying to reach me again. I need to go. I love you!"

"I love you, too." Gisella ended the call and lowered the phone. Without the adrenaline of purpose firing through her, she was left weak and lost.

Kaine had dressed in fresh jeans and a T-shirt, but he hadn't shaved. He stood with one hand on the doorjamb, the other loosely clutching his own phone.

"That's good news, isn't it?" His voice was raspy and sexy.

"That she's been released into the custody of the man who had her arrested? Sounds pretty alarming to me."

He acknowledged that with a tilt of his head. "You still want to go, then?"

Rozi wouldn't have tried to stop her getting on the plane if she wanted her to come. In fact, as Gisella thought back on the conversation, she almost thought she'd seen something in her cousin that conveyed Rozi very much preferred that Gisella *not* come. It was vestiges of something she'd seen a couple of times before, and made her prickly as she thought about it. It wasn't her fault that men sometimes looked past Rozi when Gisella showed up. Was Rozi romantically involved with Viktor? He'd had her arrested!

If Gisella hadn't slept with her own mortal enemy, she wouldn't even consider her cousin capable of it, but she had to wonder. Even if Rozi *was* sleeping with Viktor, why would she think Gisella had designs on him?

Didn't she remember that Viktor was Gisella's *cousin*?

Besides, she had no interest in other men. Kaine was the only one she wanted.

And he thought she was something between a predator and a parasite.

"Gisella? Are you okay?" He was frowning at her.

She realized she was staring at him. He'd pulled her from a fire, but she remained in a place of profound vulnerability, completely at a loss as to how to cope with what had happened between them. A few hours ago, she had hated him with every fiber of her being— but only after glorying in all the things he had made her feel. Then he'd stepped up during a potential disaster and won her over on a different level.

She snapped her gaze away from his, too raw and overwhelmed to make any sense of what she felt.

"No. I don't need to go." She didn't have to add the cost of a chartered jet to this debacle unless it was really necessary. And, somehow, she still had to make things right as far as Benny's actions went, not worse. If she started spending Kaine's money on wild-goose chases, they would remain adversaries forever.

What did she want them to be?

"I'm really sorry for all the trouble," she murmured after he finished telling his pilot to stand down.

"It keeps my staff on their toes," he said with a negligent shrug.

"I expect an invoice," she repeated. "Otherwise, I'll guess at the amount and transfer it to you."

His cheeks went hollow. "We'll talk about that later."

She didn't argue. It had been a rough night and neither of them was fit for negotiating right now.

"You should get some sleep," she told him. She ought to do the same, but felt wired, having geared herself up for travel.

"I've had half a pot of coffee. I'll be up for a while." He glanced with dismay toward the open curtains where the city was still under a blanket of darkness. "Want to go watch the sunrise?"

She choked on a laugh, then realized he was serious. They had a couple of hours before the sun came up. She was wide awake and dressed. She rarely did impulsive things like that, but always wished she were the kind of person who did. Yesterday's rain had blown itself out and the moon was playing peekaboo from behind torn clouds.

"Like, go somewhere? Or—?"

"Boardwalk at Long Beach?" he suggested.

The whole point of their being together was supposed to be a fake relationship for the benefit of others, not a sexual relationship that would start to feel awfully romantic if they chased sunrises at the beach.

Nevertheless, she reached for a thick cardigan, shrugging it over the yoga pants and long-sleeved top she'd dressed in for travel.

On impulse, she stopped him from calling his driver.

"Do you feel like driving?" She could take the wheel if he was too tired.

"You have a car?"

"Daddy does," she said with a conspirator's smile. The address of the garage was on the way and a cab was easy to flag down at this time of morning. Minutes later, she was showing her ID to the night guard, and signing out a vintage T-topped Camaro.

Kaine gave a low whistle at the apple-red sports car. "You're taking me back to my teen years, when I was boosting rides to take girls to the beach."

"I thought you only shoplifted."

"Sometimes the shop was a car lot. I always brought it back before anyone knew it was gone. Borrowing, really."

"Hmm…" She couldn't help chuckling at the distinction as they slid into the low-slung leather-covered seats.

He did like to drive. He soon had them on the freeway, where he made the engine growl as he put the car through its paces, a relaxed smile of pleasure on his face.

After a while, she filled the companionable silence with an acoustic station. She let the pluck of guitar strings drown out whatever heavy thoughts were trying to take root in her mind. For the moment, she let herself *be*. He seemed to feel the same.

When they reached Long Beach, he paid for parking and they made their way onto the boardwalk, unhurried. Streaks of orange sat on the horizon between the charcoal sky and an expanse of mottled navy blue. The tide was half out, flavoring the damp breeze with the scent of kelp and salt and all those other primordial scents that reminded her they were just two small organisms on a rock hurtling through the cosmos. The universe didn't care about their petty human anguish.

"I haven't been here since I was a kid," she said as they fell into an ambling walk. "Uncle Ben had a house here until the hurricane a few years ago. Mom and Dad usually stayed in the city, but Rozi's mom would throw me in the car with her kids and bring me out here.

It would be nothing but sunburns and junk food for days."

"I get the impression you feel fostered out in your own way."

"Do I sound self-pitying? I don't mean to. I feel really lucky to have my family."

"Because you needed them and they gave you what your parents didn't."

She faltered, pausing to set her hand on the rail. The colors on the horizon were deepening. Growing sharper and more focused.

"I'm as judgmental as the next person. Of course I think my parents could have been more emotionally accessible to me. The trade-off is that they provided for me very well. Rozi called our uncle Ben first last night, then me, because we're in a position to offer real help. Her parents would first have to book an appointment at the bank, to remortgage their house. They have always made time for their children over making money, and they had four. They struggle financially, not that they complain. They're very happy. But it creates an ironic dynamic. I'm jealous of Rozi having an ideal childhood, but she's jealous of me for all the cool stuff I had."

"Which was?"

"Anything I asked for." She shrugged it off. "When I say my parents left me to my own devices, I mean that literally."

"Ah."

She watched his gaze follow the swoop of a seagull, quite sure he had had neither his emotional nor material needs met. He had said that he stopped stealing when he was able to buy what he needed.

"The one time I remember coming to the beach as a kid, I was with a foster family. I thought they were going to leave me there." His tone was self-deprecating, but something in his expression made her quiver inside.

"Why would you think that?"

"I didn't know they wouldn't." He squinted into the distance. "I think that's why I kept getting myself sent to the lockup. I hated it there, but at least I knew what to expect. It was predictable. They told you the rules and enforced them. Going into a stranger's home, you didn't know what was going to happen next. I heard so many horror stories and was forever bracing for something bad. When a foster parent sprang a trip to the beach on me, I had every reason to assume they were going to bury me in the sand and let the tide come in."

"Kaine, that's awful." She reached to cover his cool hand.

He briefly pinched her fingers in his grip before he pushed off the rail and continued walking.

She hung back a beat, feeling rebuffed, but when she caught up to him, he caught her hand in his, squeezing again. "I don't know how to believe in people."

Her heart lurched. She was hyperaware of his warm grip on her hand and wove her fingers between his, liking the way they fit so neatly and could walk so comfortably while joined like this.

She hurt for him, though. And she understood what he was telling her, that he was trying to explain why he didn't trust her. He'd never had anyone he *could* trust.

Meanwhile, she was surrounded by people she trusted and who trusted her. That's why it was such a slap that he didn't.

She stroked the back of Kaine's knuckles, wishing she could make him see she wouldn't let him down.

He glanced at her. "Don't feel sorry for me. I'll hate it."

"I don't. I feel angry on your behalf. Guilty about Benny, even though I can't believe he would have deliberately tried to take advantage of you."

He paused at a concession stand that was opening its window. The aroma of fresh coffee wafted out along with the sugary scent of fresh doughnuts. He bought one of each for both of them and they moved to a bench, set their feet on the rail and watched the stain of purple and pink on the clouds turn red and orange at the center.

With the only sound the call of the gulls and the wash of the incoming waves, she felt as though they were the only two people on earth. It was a moment of utter peace. A few minutes later, white light broke against the horizon, beginning the new day.

Her eyes watered and she told herself it was just the long night and the beauty before her, not the poignant need to believe they were turning a corner in their relationship.

"Do you surf?" she asked as she spotted a lone nut in a wet suit being chopped up on the waves.

"I can keep myself from getting killed, but I'm not passionate about it. Do you?"

"Ha! Do you know how many points my feminist mother would give you for not simply assuming I wouldn't because I'm a girl?"

"Are you a feminist?"

"I am." She licked the last of the powdered sugar from her thumb and fingers, then dried them on her knee, saying what they had come here to talk about. "Which is why I slept with you. I wanted to, Kaine. This is my body and it was my choice to share it with you. Provided you consented, of course."

He tipped back his head and choked a laugh at the last fading star. "I consented the hell out of last night."

Indeed.

The rim of the sun became a circle, brilliant as a phoenix reborn from the ash-colored ocean. Its reflection danced toward them in a crooked line across the waves. The dark sky turned blue while the clouds faded to a delicate tangerine, pastel yellow, then creamy white.

They finished their coffee and rose to throw everything into the nearest bin.

He reached out and she let him draw her into his arms. She leaned on him, absorbing his warmth through her clothes.

"Last night was incredible, Gisella. I feel privileged that you shared your first time with me."

She closed her eyes and emotive tears stung the seam of her lashes.

"I helped Rozi because I wanted to help you. I didn't feel like you extracted anything from me. That was freely given because I like you."

Her mouth was buried against his shirt along with her closed eyes. "I'm still going to pay you back," she said, pressing away.

He sighed, but let her pull out of his arms.

They walked back to the car, but he didn't drive far. He pulled in at an office flashing "Vacancy" in a row of quaint cottages facing the water. The boutique motel had clearly been rebuilt since the storm, but was designed to look as though it had been providing seaside accommodation to upper-class families for a century.

"I need to sleep. You can leave me here if you want to."

"I'm tired, too." The coffee had done nothing to stave off the weariness catching up to her.

She could have booked her own cottage. He even glanced at her as he checked in, asking, "Would you like your own room?"

The clerk pointed out there were several beds in each one.

She went with Kaine to the end unit, where she had her choice between two queen beds and a pullout sofa, but chose the king in the loft. The ceiling was slanted and showed the beams of the peaked roof. Sunlight poured through a pair of French doors that led onto a small balcony overlooking the beach.

"That's the bed I was going to use," he said as he closed the drapes.

"I know." She shrugged out of her cardigan and stripped her yoga pants off. "I want to sleep beside you. I want the warmth of feeling you beside me. That's all I want."

He swallowed and dragged his own shirt over his head. They stripped to their underthings and crawled beneath the covers. He dragged her near-naked body into his so her cool skin was scorched by his hot chest and thighs. Then he let his heavy arms relax around her as he sighed, seeming to fall into sleep just like that.

She blinked a few times, wondering if she was giving him too much credit, but she was so content, held by him this way, she didn't examine her misgivings too closely.

She kept thinking of him as a boy, constantly having the rug pulled from beneath him. That had happened to her *once*, when her father had left. She had had an enormous safety net in her web of family, but she still carried baggage from it. He must have felt so alone, so many times.

She curled her arm around his waist, hugging herself closer against him, as if she could shield him from his own past, and nuzzled a healing kiss into his throat as she let herself drift into sleep.

CHAPTER EIGHT

GISELLA STRETCHED AS she woke, realizing there was someone against her front. Kaine. Hot. Tense. *Hard.*

"Oh," she murmured, coming fully awake in a rush.

"Yeah," he drawled, voice strained, but rueful. "We have a serious problem."

Daylight cast a muted glow upward from the open windows on the floor below. His arms were loose around her, and the shape of him against her abdomen was unmistakably, throbbingly ready for sex. She swallowed. Her own body grew tingly with arousal, making her long to slither in invitation against him.

"What—um. What's the issue?" she asked, playing dumb.

"I can't make myself leave this bed, but I

don't have a condom. So I can't stay in it. Not if you're here."

"Ah." She smirked, nose tickled by the hairs on his breastbone. "That sounds like a 'you' problem."

"Does it?" A grumble of dissatisfaction rumbled in his chest. "That's unfortunate." He glanced down at where her nipples poked with arousal against the silk cups of her bra. "I'd suggest you get up, but I don't think it'll solve anything if you walk around all sexy and beautiful."

"What if that walk takes me to my purse and I get a condom from there? Would that move us any closer to a resolution?" She used a saucy sweep of her lashes to indicate the chair in the corner.

"I like your initiative, but I have to ask." He slid a little lower in the bed, so they were nose to nose. His hand slid up her back to dislodge the strap of her bra so it loosened off the point of her shoulder. Her breasts tingled with anticipation of being bared and caressed.

'What is a virgin doing with a condom in her purse?"

"You may not have heard, but I've had to remove that particular certification from my résumé. It's a recent development."

"Did you post it to social media? They keep adjusting the algorithms. I didn't see it in my feed."

"Which explains why you don't know about the condoms. I posted a few days ago that I was going to start carrying them since a surprise kiss from a stranger had me seriously considering sex on the floor of a dead woman's parlor."

"Keep that sexy talk coming." He didn't even smile, but warmth and humor filled his gaze. "I like that you make me laugh." His deep sincerity made her heart turn over with yearning.

"Me, too," she said, trying to be flippant when she was actually so deeply moved her lips no longer felt steady.

She stroked the stubble on his cheek, thinking she maybe hadn't broken her promise to

Rozi after all. This man affected her so very deeply. She *could* love him, of that she was sure.

They exchanged a few light kisses before he suddenly rolled onto his back and threw off the covers, sending an exaggerated sigh of exasperation at the rafters. "Fine. *I'll* go.'

He made her laugh, too, fetching her purse in two strides and returning before she had even sat up.

As she opened the zipper on the inside pocket and fished out the condom, she wondered if she was crazy for letting her guard down again.

But he transfixed her as he threw himself down beside where she sat. He traced patterns across her spine, working his way toward the clasp on her bra with unhurried caresses. She held still for his tantalizing play, not caring how painful things might be in the future. *Not* making love with him right now would kill her.

She sat still until he unclipped her bra, then shrugged out of the midnight cups and threaded the straps off her arms. She threw her bra to the floor before shifting to press him onto his back and straddle him.

"Oh, it's like that, is it? One time and she thinks she's ready to take the lead."

She braced her hands on the mattress above his shoulders, head hanging so her hair fell to curtain either side of his face.

"Scared?" she mocked.

He tucked her hair behind her ear. "Terrified."

He wore a look of candor that made her laughter stop in her chest as a lump of emotion. Holding his gaze, she lowered to kiss him, desperately hoping they wouldn't destroy one another.

Kaine watched Gisella work the crowd at a political fundraiser. Along with charity galas, this type of event was where the serious wallets of Wall Street gathered in hopes of advancing their personal agendas. It was exactly the echelon he'd been trying to penetrate when her cousin's treachery had made him persona non grata.

His name had been earning narrow-eyed looks all week as he entered rooms alongside her. She faltered subtly at times. He could tell this exercise was taking a toll on her and the family name, but she had a spine of pure steel and didn't try to wriggle out of the role he'd cast her in. In fact, he almost felt as though the way she came to his defense at times was…personally motivated? Heartfelt? She seemed to genuinely want to mitigate the damage done to him by Benny.

Not that she was overt about dressing anyone down. She just smoothed over whatever asides were made with her innately cool style. He was the one who stared down the more direct attacks.

Working as a team was a unique experience for him. Every other woman had always merely hung on to his coattails while he drove his way forward. What he and Gisella were, he realized with a surprising degree of satisfaction, was a power couple. He wasn't merely double-barreled with her by his side. His standing and influence increased exponentially.

Which he shouldn't allow himself to enjoy too much. He hadn't relied on anyone since childhood. He shouldn't get used to having such an asset.

Nevertheless, he couldn't resist letting Gisella take the lead at times, not because he was uncertain how to proceed, but because she was such a kick to watch. She was like a secret weapon, deployed to make impact with a smile or a curious cant of her head. She mesmerized his opponents, put them off balance and provided him an opening to exploit at will.

Even more heady than all of that, however, was the right to set his hand on her waist and level a look at any man staring too long at her. *Mine*, he conveyed with unapologetic dominance. It didn't matter that he wore the bespoke trappings of civilized society. The barbaric possessiveness in him also doubled down the longer he was with her. He was quite willing to pick up the nearest heavy object and brain anyone who threatened what he had with her.

Which was exactly what he considered doing when they came face-to-face with Simon Walters.

"Michaels," the older man said with the same disdain he'd shown the day he had demanded new samples be analyzed from the mine site. "Gisella," Walters said more warmly, holding out a hand.

Kaine tightened his interlaced fingers over hers, preventing her from shaking.

"It's nice to see you again," she said pleasantly, flicking a glance at Kaine that questioned whether his display of antagonism was necessary.

Yes, he conveyed. Walters had been the first to pin the blame on Kaine rather than even consider that the information provided by Benny could be false.

The older man's gaze met his briefly, hostility meeting ice, then went back to Gisella's self-conscious smile.

"I've been trying to reach your uncle. Even went by the shop the other day," Walters said.

"He's been tied up with my grandmother. I haven't seen him much myself." She'd been going to work this week, but taking long lunches and slipping out early.

"Is your grandmother aware of—" Walters's gaze flicked between them "—everything that's going on?"

"Are you asking if she possesses all her faculties? Absolutely," Gisella said in a deliberated misunderstanding that made Kaine catch back an urge to laugh.

"I meant, is she aware of this association?" He nodded at Kaine.

Kaine stared grimly at the man, silently reminding Walters that he was splashing loud enough to draw the crocodile out of him.

"She's been in Florida. Why?" There was the woman who didn't back down from a fight. Kaine stroked his thumb across the back of her hand in approval.

"I think she would be interested in knowing the business she worked so hard to build is under attack."

"Barsi on Fifth has a military-grade security system."

"You take my meaning," Walters insisted through his teeth.

"I do. And I'm conveying that your concern is misplaced."

"He's angry that I bought the Garrison place. Be thankful," Kaine said to Walters. "You'd be overextended if you had won it. But it's for sale again, if you still want it."

"Yes, I've heard what you're asking for it. Robbery. Your specialty. Be careful, Gisella. Don't let him steal your reputation."

He moved away and Kaine wanted to shake him like a terrier with a rat for putting that angry, distressed look on his lover's face.

"He's being unpleasant because he was counting on me to settle the dispute and refund him in time to buy the Garrison estate, not tie up his investment in escrow and buy the estate myself. He's trying to get under my skin."

"It was a fair warning, though. We're not as resilient as you are, Kaine. Barsi on Fifth is a family-run business. We make a decent living, but it *is* our living. We can't afford to lose it." Closing her free hand into a fist at her side, she breathed a vexed, "I wish Benny would *turn up.*"

And if he did? Kaine might be exonerated, in which case Gisella would lose everything. Or Benny might have further tricks up his sleeve, revealing Gisella had been here to placate him all along.

Kaine didn't want to believe that. Nor did he want to lose her. For any reason.

"Should we go?" he said restlessly.

"Do you mind?" She sounded as tense as he was.

Without another word, he took her back to his penthouse, where he shut out the world and ravaged her mouth with his own the second they were inside the door.

She gasped in surprise at his intensity, but quickly matched it, as if she, too, sensed the sand washing away beneath their feet. She jammed her fingers into his hair and urged him to press his mouth harder against hers, until he worried he would bruise her plump lips. He scraped his teeth down her neck and her knee came up to his hip, exposing her leg through the slit in her gown.

Her hand went to his fly, squeezing him through the fabric. Her hot breath bathed his ear as she moaned with urgency.

Here? He didn't have a condom, but something feral and desperate gripped him. He jerked open his pants and heard the seam of her dress tear as he shoved it out of the way, baring her. She moved the silk of her thong aside, exposing herself to the caress of his fingertips, moans urging him on.

Soft and sleek, she parted easily under his questing touch, and arched her back as he tested the molten core of her. She whimpered as he stepped closer and rubbed his tip against her moist heat, teasing, threatening…

Then he was sliding into her, naked and stripped raw by the exquisite sensation.

He braced his forearms beside her head, his

own hanging so his temple was against the shell of her ear. He panted, blind with pleasure at the joy of being naked and squeezed by her intimate muscles. Nothing between them but a thin veil of humanity that kept him this side of sane.

Her calf pressed against his ass, urging him deeper, while her hands shifted across the back of his shirt beneath his jacket. He was on fire, so hot he was sweating. He wanted to tear every stitch from both of them, but he needed this more. *Her.* Moving and feeling every twinge of her response. Listening to the break in her breath and tasting the lascivious passion on her tongue.

He couldn't come in her like this. He knew he couldn't, but he pumped his hips, longing to go all the way. Desperate to feel her shatter. Needing her surrender like air.

"You're mine." He turned his head to whisper the words directly into her ear. "I'm going to have you so many ways, you'll forget what it's like not to belong to me. No one else is ever going to give you this."

"I know," she gasped, neck arched as she offered herself to each of his thrusts.

"Open your eyes." He cupped her face, looking into the glazed sheen of green, watched her parted lips tremble as he deliberately slowed his thrusts, drawing out the pleasure. "Do you want me to come with you?"

His scalp tingled as he asked it. He wanted to put a baby in her. Bind her to him forever. The idea ought to terrify him, but he was feeling primitive enough to glory in the thought of a lifelong bond between them.

Her brow wrinkled in agony. He could feel the subtle signals in her embrace that urged him to keep making love to her, but he refused, only held her on that precipice. Her breath was jagged and the way she was squeezing him meant she was very close. So was he. A few thrusts and both their lives could change forever.

"Together?" he asked.

Shadows crept in to douse the arousal that fogged her gaze.

It was a tiny, tiny rejection, but it went

through him like a blade, clean and sharp, severing a delicate silken thread he hadn't even realized had bound him to her.

With great care, he withdrew. The pain of it was like flaying his own skin from his body. He ignored the burn. There was plenty of scar tissue to replace it.

"Bedroom, then."

Seconds later, he had his barrier in place and thrust into her again, well protected this time and trying to convince himself he was glad.

CHAPTER NINE

GISELLA HAD BEEN CLOSE, *so close*, to having unprotected sex. Hell, they had had unprotected sex! He just hadn't…

She was twenty-four and children were still very much a someday thing for her. She would never, ever, *ever* use a baby to trap a man. Not only was it an awful thing to do to a partner and a child, her mother had drilled into her that the one who was trapped when a baby came along was a woman. That attitude of resentment contributed to their sometimes strained relationship and Gisella's struggle to believe in romantic love. Given her parents' divorce, she knew better than anyone that a baby didn't *keep* a couple together.

Still, there had been a moment, a single pulse beat, when she had been intimately joined with Kaine and had yearned for a tie that would last a lifetime.

Sanity had prevailed, but she was thinking of picking up a morning-after pill, just to be sure. Kaine might have been as reckless as she was in those few seconds of naked sex, but she knew who would carry the blame if a long-odds touchdown occurred. Would he marry her if she turned up pregnant? She rather thought his upbringing would compel him to, but she would be subject to his suspicions for however long their union lasted.

And it wouldn't last. Because she wouldn't be able to stand his lack of trust.

"Nice try," Kaine said under his breath, adding an epithet.

"Pardon?" Gisella dragged herself back to the penthouse and breakfast and the fact her bare soles were stacked on the tops of Kaine's warm feet beneath the table. His robe was askew, exposing the crisp hairs on his chest.

"Oh. Okay, then," Kaine said, seeming appeased as he read further in his email. "Viktor Rohan sent me some money. I thought he was making presumptions about my desire to sell the earring, but it's for your cousin's legal fees."

"Are you accepting it?"

"Yes."

"Why?"

"Because I don't want that debt between you and me."

"Hmm…" She tightened her mouth.

"You do?" His dark brows went up.

"No. But I don't want her to feel in debt to *him*. You said yourself he's a man with a lot of power."

"He is." Kaine clicked off his phone. "What's going on between them? Have you spoken with her?"

"I've tried. The time difference has made it awkward, but I feel like she's putting me off." It wasn't like Rozi to keep secrets from her. "I even resorted to…" She hesitated, then wrinkled her nose and admitted, "We had a secret code when we were in middle school. We used it if we needed to get out of an invitation or wanted to cut class."

"You cut classes in middle school? You're sounding more and more like my kind of girl."

"It was more about seeing if we could get away with it. We never did," she said with a rueful chuckle. "We'd sit in the girls' room, bored, not even smoking because Grandpapa died of lung cancer so we wouldn't even consider it. Then our absence would be reported to our parents and Rozi's mom would say something like, *Were you not feeling well, darling? Call me anytime. I'll come get you.* Meanwhile, *my* mother would lecture me. 'African girls are starving for the education you're throwing away.'"

He quirked a brow.

"True story."

"What was the code?"

"I can't tell you! It's a secret. What if I want to get away from *you*?" Beneath the table, she slid her feet around his ankle.

He leaned forward and captured her wrists in each of his hands, kissing her pulse in the tender underside of each. "Why would you want to do that?"

She wouldn't. She didn't.

"Rozi didn't want an excuse to leave Rohan?"

She had to concentrate to remember what they were talking about. "She said they were on their way to visit Viktor's great-aunt. Istvan's sister."

"She's still alive? How old is she?"

"Eighty-one, same as Grandmamma."

"Why does she want to see her?"

Gisella shook her head. "That's Rozi. She'll be in her element, traveling into the country to interview an elderly relative."

"Not your thing."

Not if she could sit here being seduced over scrambled eggs, but… She licked her lips. They tingled as his gaze followed the motion.

"Is it yours?" she asked. "Because my grandmother is home from Florida. I ought to go visit her. I'd like to introduce you, if you're willing."

"Why?" He released her and sat back. Even his feet disappeared from beneath hers.

"I don't want her to hear from someone else that I'm dating. She would expect me to introduce you if we were…" She swallowed. "Serious. I can't tell her anything about Benny. That would—"

"I understand." His expression was enigmatic. "Of course. Today?"

She nodded. "I'll call to make sure she's up for it."

Kaine was feeling quite the hypocrite. He had reflexively withdrawn from Gisella's desire to introduce him to her grandmother, then he'd been offended that it was another facet of their ruse.

Did he *want* her to introduce him as a genuine suitor? No. He had given up thinking of family ties as anything but a hindrance years ago, certainly not something he wanted or needed.

Nevertheless, the more he witnessed Gisella's attachment to her family, the more he was drawn in by that web. She lit up at any communication from one of them. It might be only some banter with one of her younger cousins about a movie or a recipe from her aunt, but it made him wonder what it was like to be included in her world.

"Your grandmother lives alone?" he asked when they arrived in front of a well-kept older building.

"All of us have invited her at different times to live with us. Will you forgive me if I gloss over the part about staying with you? She's old-fashioned."

He stopped himself from asking why the woman who'd been pregnant and unmarried held others to higher standards.

"And don't mention the earring. She won't talk about something so personal with a stranger."

"Would you like me to excuse myself so you can ask her about it?"

"You wouldn't mind?"

"No. But how will I know when it's appropriate to leave without insulting her?"

Gisella's mouth twitched into a pert smile. She knew he was asking about her secret code with Rozi. With a groan of capitulation, she tugged her earlobe.

"It's this, okay? Sometimes we say, 'Did you lose your earring?' or 'Did you find your earring?' But the joke was on me with Rozi this week. We were texting and it turned into a *Who's on First?* routine with her saying, 'Viktor has it,' every time I asked." She rolled her eyes in exasperation. "She finally said, all caps, 'My earrings are totally fine.'"

"And your family has never figured out this extremely sophisticated ploy?"

"I know, right?" She led him out of the elevator and down three doors where she knocked briefly, then tapped a code into an electronic door lock. "It's me," she called as they entered. "Oh, it smells good in here."

The aroma of fresh bread with cinnamon was layered over the scent of strong coffee and the dry heat of a well-warmed apartment. He wished he wasn't wearing a suit, but Gisella had insisted he dress as though attending a high-stakes business meeting. As her grandmother appeared, he understood why.

"They're from frozen, but they're your auntie's, so they'll be good," Ezti Barsi said in a heavily accented voice.

The octogenarian moved slowly from the galley kitchen, but she was the epitome of old-world elegance. She wore a collared jacket over a skirt, pearls, lipstick and neatly coiffed white hair. She looked ready to attend a wedding at an orthodox church, complete with polished dress shoes that had a low, chunky heel.

The women exchanged a warm embrace, kissing each other's cheeks before Gisella drew back to introduce him.

"So handsome." Ezti pinched his cheek.

Gisella buried a snicker into her scarf and took over preparing the coffee and rolls while he waited for her grandmother to lower into an armchair before taking a seat on the love seat.

She grilled him without apology, wanting to know where he came from, how they'd met, what he did for a living and why he was in New York.

He didn't see a lot of Gisella in her physically, but the sharp wit and lack of intimidation had definitely been passed along to her granddaughter. It was a perfectly pleasant half hour.

Eventually, she turned her attention to other matters, saying to Gisella, "Your aunt said Rozi is having the time of her life, but I know when my children are keeping something from me. You'll tell me the truth, won't you?"

"Always, Grandmamma. And Rozi is fine. I've been in touch with her, but there was a small incident." Gisella's hand went to her ear self-consciously.

Kaine took the hint and rose. "I've just remembered. You wanted new earbuds. I saw an electronics store down the block. I'll run and get those while I'm thinking of it."

As Kaine left, Gisella's grandmother repeated, "Earbuds?"

"The things you put in your ears to listen to music," Gisella explained in Hungarian.

"He must be something if you're teaching

him your secret code." *Nothing* got by this woman. "How did you meet him?"

She led with her attempt to buy the earring at auction and got as far as Rozi going after Viktor's in Hungary. By that point, her grandmother was becoming quite agitated.

"We thought it would be a nice surprise for you," Gisella said, pleading for understanding. "You've always been so sad when you talk about Istvan. We wanted you to at least have the gift he gave you."

"I had your mother. That's always been enough for me. Tell Rozi to let it rest," she said firmly.

Gisella promised she would pass that message along and changed the topic to something less volatile while she cleaned up their dishes. She met up with Kaine a short while later.

Since it was a gorgeous day and they were only two blocks away, he arranged to meet his driver on the other side and they walked through Central Park. The city fell away and the scent of spring filled her nostrils. Trees were coated in pastel blossoms and couples made out amid the wildflowers beneath them. Families pushed strollers and set out picnics while dog walkers tried to keep their clients from charging after the chattering squirrels.

She needed this restorative moment. Her heart was heavy.

"I upset my grandmother," she admitted. "I feel awful. I think the earring became our personal treasure hunt, more about our ability to retrieve it. We told ourselves we were doing it for Grandmamma, but we just stirred up old heartache. My mother was right and I should have grown out of this quest a long time ago."

Kaine slid her a sideways look. "What does that mean? I went to a lot of trouble myself for that earring. Now you don't want it?"

"You can sell it to Viktor Rohan." She hugged his arm. "When I get hold of Rozi, I'll tell her to give up on his. Let his mother have both."

"You're serious. You don't want it."

She watched his skepticism turn to confusion. Part of him had still thought she was sleeping with him for the earring, she realized, and she let go his arm.

"It's not worth the hurt it's causing. Grandmamma was so upset to learn about Rozi being arrested."

"You told her about that?"

"I had to! It's my fault Rozi was there. I was supposed to go and we switched at the last minute. I thought Grandmamma was going to get the wooden spoon," Gisella muttered.

"She hits you?" His outrage was palpable.

"No! No, it's just something she would threaten sometimes when one of us was out of line. It's a family joke to say that. It means we know we screwed up."

He had left his jacket in the car and his shoulders remained tense beneath the cut of his shirt. She eyed him.

"Did—?" She wasn't sure she could bear to know that someone had ever hit him.

"Once," he said quietly. "With a belt. I was moved right away. To the family that took me to the beach."

She swallowed. No wonder he had been terrified by something that should have been a fun outing.

"That's when…" He trailed off.

They had reached the pond. On the far side, a dad was showing his kids how to run the controls on a pair of remote control toy speedboats.

Kaine shoved his hands deep into his pockets. "That's when I asked about my mother's family. I'd been in care for a couple of years. I was old enough to know there might be a chance at something else. Something…real. I nagged for them to see what they could find out. The social worker told me they had already been in contact with my mother's sister and they had financial problems. A sick kid. They couldn't help me."

It didn't matter that it sounded like a legitimate excuse. Maybe they hadn't even been allowed to take him on, under those circumstances. She still felt his pain at having his young hopes dashed.

"They didn't even ask to see you?"

"No."

He had taken an emotional chance and lost. No wonder he refused to take any more.

"You never tried to reach out to them?"

"They sent a note a couple of years ago. An invitation to a *quinceañera* for—I guess she'd be my cousin? I had just been featured in a list of California's richest tech billionaires. It was obvious what they wanted. I sent a check and my regrets. I haven't heard from them since."

Maybe they hadn't known how to find him until they saw him in the news. She wanted to suggest there was still time to form ties, persuade him that cousins were as good as siblings in a lot of ways, but her throat ached too much. She could see he would rather put up a wall than open a door.

"I look at you with your family and it's like watching a foreign film," he said with a shake of his head.

"In Hungarian?" She tried to lighten things up.

"Yeah." His mouth twitched. "Without subtitles. It's one of the hardest languages to learn

Did you know that? I looked it up," he said in a self-deprecating aside.

She knew he was throwing that out as a joke, but she was touched that he would take that step of curiosity. It sounded as if he wanted to know more about her, have a future where he spoke her mother tongue. But she also read the subtext in what he was saying, too. Family was beyond his ability to grasp.

Gisella entered Kaine's Manhattan office with one hand stifling a yawn and sank into the sofa that faced a wall-mounted television. She thumped her bag onto the floor beside her, but kept the coffee she had picked up on her way from the shop.

"TGIF," she declared. "My dad has offered us his courtside tickets if you want to use them tonight. But I don't know how much longer I can keep this up. I never go out this much."

"Do you like basketball?"

"Not particularly, but if your goal is to be seen with me, the game is going to be televised. There's a restaurant on the way where paparazzi hang out looking for celebs."

He came from behind his desk and she tilted her head back to look at him, expecting him to ask whether they should go home and change or some other logistical question.

Instead, he showed her a velvet box. It was faded but wore a gold stamp that was an elaborate, primitive version of the one stamped onto the boxes that her own pieces were sold in.

"Were you serious when you said you no longer want this?"

She realized her mouth hung open and clamped it shut, then set down her coffee and picked up her feet as she twisted on the sofa.

"I don't—I mean, if you're asking whether I want to buy it—" If he offered to give it to her, she would *die*. "No. I don't want it for myself or my grandmother. But..." She started to tremble the way she had as a little girl, when it was Christmas morning and she had to contain herself. "Please, can I look at it?"

Something passed behind his eyes. "Of course." He continued holding it out to her.

Had this been a test? Had she passed? She took the box, then sent a pinched frown up at him. "Are you telling me this was never in a safe-deposit box? You've had it on you all this time?"

He only shrugged.

She tsked, then took her time with the big reveal, gently prying against the lid to ease it open. He stood over her, able to see how much she was shaking.

She laughed self-consciously. "These old boxes can snap shut and take your finger off— Oh..."

The satin bed was revealed and there it was.

The photograph hadn't done it justice at all. The beaded granulation in the gold that rimmed the clover shape was exquisitely crafted. Even without her loupe, she could see the slight imperfection in the cut of the four square-cut blue sapphires, but it gave it such character, such depth. Dozens of diamonds no bigger than a twentieth of a carat sat in rose settings and formed petal patterns around the oval sapphire in the center. A second, slightly smaller blue gem hung from the bottom, framed in more of the intricate beadwork.

"The paperwork says she wore it as a scarf pin sometimes," Kaine said. "Before the pin broke off."

The backing of the earring was missing, which was why it had been locked away, she supposed. Such a shame. It was a beautiful piece, obviously made with the greatest of care.

She absently shifted so she could reach for her purse. A moment later she had her loupe and a notebook. She settled in to start sketching and making notes, adjusting the lamp on the end table so the light fell where she needed it.

"I guess we're not going to the game," Kaine said drily.

"Hmm?" She lifted her head.

"Nothing. Would you like a drink?"

"Coffee is fine," she murmured, and promptly

forgot about it as she fell into the artistry of a long-ago craftsman's opus.

Ages later, she came out of what felt like a meditative state to see Kaine sitting in an armchair, a look of bemused interest on his face.

"Am I boring you to tears?" She realized she'd been schooling him on metallurgy and the mysterious technique used by ancient Etruscans.

"Am I crying?"

"I get passionate about my work sometimes. I know how finicky and time-consuming it is to get the effect I want with modern methods. I can't believe they were able to do such so-phisticated things with such primitive tools." She nestled the earring back in its case and offered it back to him.

He took his time leaning forward to accept it, watching her.

"It's okay," she said truthfully, stomach still fluttery with excitement, but she was coming down from her high. She had taken photos and felt a lot of things in giving up the desire to own it, but not regret. "It was enough to see it."

He set it on the side table at his elbow.

"Thank you." She rose and moved to straddle him in the armchair. "This was the best date you've ever taken me on."

"So easy to please." He set his hands on her hips. "You were funny to watch. Your tongue comes out the corner of your mouth when you're sketching."

"I know," she groaned, ducking her head into his shoulder. "Rozi teases me all the time. But seriously, thank you." She shifted to stroke his shoulders and kiss him lightly, then drew back to smooth her hands on his cheeks, growing solemn. "I'm glad to give it up, if you want the truth. I hate that you ever thought I would sleep with you for it. Now you know I only want you."

He didn't react beyond a shift of his gaze as he weighed her statement.

"Of course, if you want me to express my appreciation for letting me hold it…" She tried to lighten the mood by slinking her hand between them to squeeze the flesh firming in his lap. "Hold *this*, I mean. Not the earring."

His mouth twitched while his expression became the relaxed yet intent one that told her desire had its hooks in him.

"You don't owe me anything for showing it to you." He shifted his legs beneath her, though, making it easier for her to fondle him. "The earring, I mean. Or *that*."

"It was a sweet thing to do," she said, unable to keep from growing serious. In the couple of weeks they'd been together, they had taken to leaving a lot unsaid between them, preferring to lose themselves in sensuality without having the hard conversations that might impact their pleasure.

She couldn't hold him like this, though, and look into his eyes and pretend that she wasn't moved by his wanting to make her happy, even if only for an hour.

The earring might have brought her to him, Benny's situation might have kept her with him, but this... This wasn't about any of that.

As she stroked him, she knew this was

about *them*. She began to tremble in a different way, from deep emotions that were intimate and raw. She was making the advances here and felt vulnerable in doing it. As though her heart was unprotected and open. He could reach out and break it with a breath of well-chosen words.

Her throat grew hot and pressure gathered in her chest.

"I'm not trying to thank you or anything," she said in a husky whisper. "I'm just really happy. You knew I would like it and you sat there and let me be myself, all obsessive and everything. It makes me feel…" Like she was inching onto a very delicate, new and green limb. Would it support the weight of everything that was between them? Bend? Snap? "I don't know how to express how I feel except to get close to you. Naked close."

"I'm always happy to be naked with you. You know that."

His voice was a low rumble, affected by the way she was caressing him through his pants. He was hard as iron beneath her touch, which made her own loins tingle with desire for the shape of him thrusting deep within her. Neither of them was breathing steadily.

But she could feel him still holding up that wall between them. Maybe she was so acutely aware of it because hers had come down. She didn't even have a velvet curtain or a silken veil. The last of her fortifications were gone because, she realized with astonishment, she had fallen in love with him.

The emotion washed over her in a wave, as though she'd been holding it behind her own inner dam and, now that the barriers were gone, she was submerged in her feelings for him. Drowning in them.

She cupped his strong jaw and kissed him, poured herself into it so he jerked back to look at her with a stunned light in his eyes before dragging her back into the kiss and returning her passion with equal intensity.

It spurred her on. Made her believe this giant feeling overwhelming her was returned. She ran her hands over his neck and shoulders while her hips followed the rhythm he set with his grasp of her hips, rocking her against him while they kissed.

Slow down, she thought. Love was supposed to be romantic, not frantic, but there was something desperate in both of them. Threatened. She was brazen, pushing her tongue without inhibition between his lips. He returned her flagrant passion, skimming his hands up beneath her top to cup her breasts through her bra.

They made love constantly. Her nipples were tender from his regular stimulation of them, but he mercilessly teased them through silk and lace, making her moan in pleasure-pain.

That's what all of this was. Pleasure-pain. The pleasure was here, the pain was stalking them like a bloodthirsty animal.

She dragged at his shirt, needing his naked chest.

"Wait," he bit out, then lifted his hips beneath hers to draw a condom from his pants pocket. He clamped it in his teeth, then threw off his shirt.

She scraped teeth and nails across his chest, found his beaded nipples and tortured them, making his breath hiss and his hips rise into her, threat and promise at once.

He skimmed her own top up, forcing her to lift her arms. Then he was stealing her bra while she took the condom and folded her arms behind his neck. They were chest to chest, the brush of naked skin a relief yet inciting. They kissed with ferocity, nearly savage in their hunger.

She knew they should slow down, but *Don't leave me. Don't let this end.* That's all she could think.

His hands went down her back into the waistband of her jeans, snugly cupping her butt and squeezing in the way that always made her squirm with excitement. She went up on her knees and he had her nipples now. He sucked hard, sending sharp sensations deep into her core. She cradled his head in her arms, buried her nose in his hair to drink in his scent and bit at the top of his ear.

When he dropped his head back, his lips

were pulled back against his teeth in strain, the glitter in his eyes atavistic.

She responded to it, rising to peel off her jeans while he skimmed his own pants down and kicked them away. When they were naked, she returned to straddle his thighs. She rolled the condom on and positioned herself, sank onto him and groaned her relief at the ceiling.

He shifted lower, so she could sink deeper onto him. They were joined as tightly as possible and only then were they able to slow things down. They kissed again. For a long time they only kissed, not moving except to caress and break for a gasped breath and tilt their heads the other way.

Now, she thought. Now they were making love. Her love for him emanated from every fiber of her being. She wanted to say it, but the words were superfluous. The emotion saturated every movement they made.

He pulsed inside her as their tongues played. She squeezed him when he traced the cleft of her cheeks. She dropped her face to his neck and he tenderly brushed her hair back from her face. She grazed her lips across his brow. He caressed a tickling touch in her lower back, causing her to arch in their first abbreviated thrust.

They wallowed in the act, gazing into each other's eyes as they moved together, finding the rhythm that held them in that state of shared ecstasy.

Here was the love she had looked for all her life, the one she had wanted to believe existed. Here was the man who added something new to her life she hadn't known she needed. It wasn't just the physical pleasure, but the swelling of her heart, the glory of giving him everything he needed. Being something more together than they could be as individuals.

He was holding her hips, rising to meet her, keeping their stare locked so they were exactly matched in their climb to the peak. Both of them damp and trembling, holding back, yet urging the other, closer, closer, right there…

And then it was upon them, binding them together in a moment that tasted like forever.

Later that night, long after he had put the earring into his safe at work and picked up takeout Italian on their way back to this penthouse, Kaine lay awake on his back, Gisella tucked into his side under his arm, soft and smooth and naked. Her head was heavy enough on his shoulder that he would get pins and needles soon, but he didn't move. The weight of her arm rested across his stomach, her thigh was crooked over his. Her hair tickled his chin and her breasts were that unique, delightful pressure against his rib cage that only a woman's breasts could be. Her breathing told him she had settled into a deep sleep.

He should get some sleep himself. It was after midnight, but he knew his nights of holding her like this were finite. He was determined to enjoy them to the fullest while he could.

If she knew how often he lay awake like this, memorizing the feel of her, the scent in her hair, soothing her if she happened to twitch, resisting the urge to run his hands over every inch of her soft skin so he wouldn't wake her, she would think him insane.

He was insane. Cracking up. Definitely the forged and tempered core of him had been fractured and weakened by this woman, especially now that she had so firmly decided against wanting the earring.

Sell it to Viktor Rohan, she had said. He hadn't quite believed her. Part of him had maintained the belief all along that acquiring the earring was her *real* reason for sleeping with him. He had decided almost immediately after they began sharing a bed that he would give her the earring when they parted.

Now, even after holding it and clearly being entranced by it, she still didn't want it. She'd even told him flat out that she preferred it not be between them, muddying what they had.

What *did* they have? He had thought he had a mistress right up until this evening when their always intense and satisfying sex had turned a corner into something that had felt… different. Profound.

It had shaken him to his core. He'd wanted to retreat afterward, yet hadn't been able to. Physically, he'd been too weak to move. She'd sat boneless upon him while they both recovered, but even when they moved to dress and leave, he hadn't been able to let her step beyond touching distance without dragging her close for another kiss.

Facing a boisterous crowd at a game was out of the question. He'd brought her back here, where they spent the evening on the couch, just being together. They shared a bottle of wine and rich pasta, kissing randomly, limbs draped across each other like puppies in a basket. It had been positively indolent.

It had been a disarming type of bliss. He shouldn't be relaxing his guard this way. He was leaving a flank open. That scared the hell out of him.

A buzzing came to his ears. His phone in the other room was vibrating on the table where he'd left it. He ignored it and shifted carefully, trying to get some blood flow into his arm without disturbing her.

He couldn't keep this up. He'd written off long-term relationships years ago for a reason, having learned there was no such thing as permanence or even commitment. The more attached he grew, the greater the agony when he lost.

The doorman's line on the bedside table jangled, startling him. Gisella jolted awake with a gasp.

"It's just the phone," he told her, giving her a quick squeeze of reassurance before reaching for it, cutting it off in the middle of a second jarring ring.

It was the middle of the night. *"What?"* he said flatly, conveying his dismay.

"I am so sorry, sir. It's Kelly, the doorman. There's a man here insisting you're expecting him. Benedek Barsi?"

Kaine swore. "Let him up."

He flung himself from the bed and reached for his pants, blocking out by habit any conjecture as to what this meant for him and

Gisella. He already knew it would be bad. It always was. Maybe it would be exactly what he needed to make a clean break.

"Did I hear that right?" she murmured, sounding half-asleep even as she rose to search out her own clothes. "Is Benny downstairs?"

"Sounds like it."

"How does he even know where to find you?"

"He emailed earlier this week."

Gisella paused in closing her bra between her breasts. "Why didn't you tell me?"

"That's all there is to tell. I didn't know when he would arrive. Didn't believe he would dare show his face."

"You still could have told me." She dragged a light turtleneck over jeans and pulled her hair free. "But you still don't trust me," she surmised, turning to pick up a hairbrush.

He heard the hurt in her tone, saw the stiffness in her back and bit back a sigh. He *couldn't*. Even if his head would let him, his heart didn't know how.

The ping of the elevator arriving on the top floor sounded beyond the lounge door. Kaine crossed through the penthouse to open the door before Benny had to knock.

Like Gisella, Benny was tall, but the obvious similarities ended there. Benny's hair was dark brown, not caramel, his jaw wider, his mouth nothing like the feminine bow that Gisella's was. Benny's eyes were dark brown where hers were green.

His gaze unlocked from Kaine's and moved beyond him as Gisella appeared.

"Gisella." He was taken aback. "What are you doing here?" Comprehension struck just as quickly. His gaze shot back to Kaine's, whip fast and full of outrage. "Are you kidding me?"

"Ben," Gisella said in a conciliatory tone, moving across to offer a light kiss on his cheek. "It's not what you think."

"It's exactly what I think." Benny drilled his contempt into Kaine's deliberately flat stare as he swept his arm out and tried to maneuver Gisella behind his back.

Barbaric possessiveness unlike any Kaine had ever known growled in him. *Mine.* He narrowed his eyes on Benny while a metallic taste arrived on his tongue.

But he'd been here before. He had already lost her. Whatever he had thought they had would evaporate into thin air now. He would be in the back of a car, alone, going somewhere else, very soon.

"Don't go all big brother," Gisella said with a light shove of annoyance against Benny's arm, not letting him block her from Kaine. "Come and sit down. Tell us what is going on. Do you want me to make coffee?"

"No," both men said in unison.

"Look at that. You two agree on something." She smiled despite a tension so thick, the room seemed encased in gelatin. She felt trapped and suffocated, yet quivering and fragile.

"Gisella, *what* are you doing here?" Benny asked through his teeth.

She tilted her head, willing her cheeks not to go red, silently asking, *What do you think?*

"What about Rozi?"

"Oh, for God's sake," she groaned at the ceiling, wishing they had never *proudly* announced to their family they had made their childish pact. And she was going really red now because she *was* in love, exactly as she and Rozi had sworn they should be with their first.

She probably should have said it to Kaine earlier this evening. She'd felt so close to him all night, as though they were two halves of a whole.

Maybe she had sensed that he wasn't ready to fully trust her because she had held back saying the words aloud and, moments ago, he had revealed he definitely didn't trust her. She was still aching at that. Wanting more time with him to close up that fissure between them.

"I'm an adult and can sleep with whomever I want without asking *any* of my cousins to sign off." She flicked a glance at Kaine, wanting him to hear the subtext. What they had was purely between them. It had nothing to do with anyone else.

He remained unreadable.

"Not him, Gizi," Benny said with a dark scowl. "Not like this. For God's sake, man," Benny said with disgust. "She's a twenty-four-year-old kid."

"Hey." Gisella grabbed Benny's arm and gave it a firm shake. "*I'm standing right here.* Don't talk about me like I'm not. Especially don't talk about me like I'm too young to hear bad news or too dim to understand the implications."

"He's using you as leverage, Gizi. *Insurance* to put pressure on me."

She snapped a look at Kaine, wanting him to deny it. Her presence at his side might have started out that way, but, "That's not what this is." She heard the quaver in her voice. They were so much closer now. Weren't they?

Kaine seemed to gather himself in a way that chilled her blood. As though he was bracing himself to do something difficult.

"What is it, then?" Benny demanded. "If you've fallen in love, you should have known better. I can guarantee he hasn't. Have you? Are your intentions honorable?" Benny asked Kaine with thick sarcasm.

"Benny, don't." Something as new as what they had couldn't withstand that much poking and prodding. It would break.

But she suddenly heard Kaine's warning to her that night in San Francisco. *I'll take whatever you offer, but I won't give you anything in return.* At no point had he pretended they had a future. She felt so empty in that moment, she could hardly hold on to her composure.

"I told you I was going to straighten this out," Benny spat at him. "You didn't have to go after my family."

"You dropped off the face of the earth. She showed up." Kaine's shoulders bunched, ready to fend off an attack.

"He had Grandmamma's earring," Gisella explained when Benny snapped her a look.

"Still with that?"

"I don't want it anymore so it doesn't even matter." She looked to Kaine. Didn't her giving up that earring mean anything to him? She had thought that, at least, had proved something.

"Kaine had it and I went to make an offer. That's when he told me there was a problem with some mineral samples. Benny…"

It was Benny's turn to struggle with some internal demon. She watched the pressure build in him. Fury hissed out of him on a breath. He ran a hand over his hair.

"Mistakes were made. I trusted the wrong person. It wasn't intentional, but I'm to blame. I'll be taking full responsibility." He turned back to Kaine. "I *told* you that in my email. The press release has already gone out exonerating you and your company. It's on the overseas wires if you want to read it."

Kaine moved to pick up his phone.

"What does it say?" Gisella asked with sick dread.

"Exactly what I just said. It's bad, Gizi." He rubbed the back of his neck. "I called Dad on the way here, warned him that Barsi Minerals won't survive. I don't know about the shop."

"You mean…" She searched his gaze, ears ringing, equilibrium threatening to fail her. 'Barsi on Fifth might fold? What *happened*?"

He closed his eyes, shutting her out, but she read his remorse and anguish. "How it happened doesn't matter. I have to own up to it and make reparations. Return the investors' money, submit to an investigation and pay fines. Otherwise, I'll wind up in jail. I'm ruined." He pinched the bridge of his nose.

Kaine clicked off his phone, the sound overloud in the stunned silence.

Benny lifted his head to say an antagonistic, "Satisfied?"

Kaine was so terribly remote. He still wasn't looking at her, which made her heart judder in her chest.

"Get your things, Gisella," Benny said gently.

"No. Kaine—"

"He needs to distance himself now, *unokatest-*

vér." Cousin. "Our name is mud. He can't risk being associated any longer."

"Kaine?" She heard the plea in her voice, the complete lack of pride.

"I'll get your things from my room," he said quietly, heading down the hallway. "You still have some clothes in the guest room. Your suitcase is there."

She followed him into his room and closed the door. "This doesn't have to change anything."

"It has already changed everything." He opened a drawer and scooped out her underthings, tossing them onto the bed. A pair of jeans from the next drawer down followed.

"Benny is taking full responsibility! I won't beg you for leniency because there's none you can offer. You don't have anything I want except *you*. I love you, Kaine."

Her heart beat outside her body, way out at the end of her outstretched arm, on the hem of her sleeve. It hurt, drawn with tension as it was pulled out of her center in offering, vulnerable as a freshly hatched chick.

It especially hurt to watch his expression shutter.

"He said the shop will suffer," he reminded her.

"Don't." She pulled her fist in against her cold, hollow chest. "Don't you dare accuse me of that. Is that really what you think of me? That I would ask you to bail us out? That that's what I want from you after everything I've…" …*given you.*

For a moment, she had to breathe, just breathe.

"Don't you trust me at all?" she asked, voice thin and rasped by the pain racking through her. "Don't you feel anything toward me? *Want* me?"

"I can't afford to." He set her phone, earbuds and charger on her clothes.

"I have never wanted *things*, Kaine. I want hearts. Affection. *Love.* If you can't offer me that, fine. But if you think all anyone could want from you is your material assets, then you don't appreciate your own value. And you should. Because you are worth loving."

He piled everything atop the jeans and held them out to her. "Goodbye, Gisella."

Drawing a breath that sawed like a knife in her lungs, she took it with shaky hands.

He moved into the lounge while she carried it to the other room.

She heard Benny say: "This wasn't necessary. She had nothing to do with this. *Nothing.* No matter what she says about making her own decisions, you know damned well you took advantage of her. Un. Cool."

She strained her ears, but Kaine made no response.

When she returned to the lounge, her heart was a hot red coal in her chest, burning against the back of her breastbone, making her shoulders flex in agony.

Kaine stood with his back to Benny, staring out the window.

For some reason, she thought of the dark night when he had stepped up to help Rozi. For her. It had ended in watching the sunrise together, marking the dawn of something she had believed was precious and beautiful and real.

Benny took her bag and her arm.

She couldn't bring herself to say goodbye. She left without saying anything.

CHAPTER TEN

KAINE WENT BACK to San Francisco and waited. He watched and he waited. First Benny's subsidiary, Barsi Minerals, dominated the headlines with the scandalous admission of fraud. As Benny had predicted, the company took a massive drubbing in the financial pages. It was killed, plucked, roasted and chewed down to the bone within hours. Valued lower than nuclear waste.

On the entertainment sites, where Benny had been one of New York's most eligible bachelors, he was now labeled the black sheep of the Barsi family.

To Kaine's surprise, they didn't distance themselves. The smart thing would have been for Barsi on Fifth to renounce him, but a newscaster spoke over footage of Benny and his father helping Gisella's grandmother from a town car before going into the offices of a top defense lawyer.

They would go broke keeping Benny from doing hard time, but didn't seem to care.

Kaine had also been keeping an eye on the valuation on Gisella's father's company. It, too, was dropping without a parachute. Drummond's association to the Barsi family, and her recent affair with Kaine, had scared away a number of her father's best clients.

Attempts were made by entertainment rags to drag Kaine and his company onto the scandal sheets, but his PR department characterized his affair with Gisella as a "brief association" regarding another matter. His team made clear statements that he'd been misled by Barsi Minerals along with the rest of the investors. Riesgo Ventures expected payments for damages in due course.

With his own funds freed up from the escrow, he was at full speed again. In fact, Walters and the rest of the investors crawled back, eager to speculate in rare metals with him if he found an honest geologist this time. He gave the whole thing to one of his executives and told him to come back with a proposal. His personal interest in that topic had waned.

Was that what he and Gisella had had? A "brief association"?

Against every rational thought in his brain, he had started to consider offering help that night. She hadn't let him. She didn't want *things*.

If you think all anyone could want from you is your material assets, then you don't appreciate your own value. You are worth loving.

Of all the things he dared not trust, that was probably the biggest. Life was far easier to bear if he believed that love was a fantasy. It wasn't something he should expect because it wasn't real. Therefore he felt no disappointment in never receiving any.

I love you, Kaine.

Why did it hurt to hear that? Why did it hurt *so much*?

He stared with sightless eyes out his glass office overlooking the bay. Behind him, on his Italian-designed, ultracontemporary desk, sat a faded velvet box. He kept thinking that if he had insisted she take that damned earring, she could have sold it to Rohan by now. It would give her family some extra cash to weather this storm. Benny would have to take his lumps, but at least the rest of her family would be insulated.

He had looked up Rohan to see if his "brief association" bailing Rozalia out of jail was making headlines. If it was, they weren't in English. If Rozi was prevailing on Rohan for financial assistance for the family, that wasn't obvious, either. As far as Kaine could tell, that pair had gone underground. He checked the social media sites and there was no indication that Rozi was back in New York.

That had to be bothering Gisella. Dismissive as he might be of that elusive emotion love, he knew she felt it toward her cousin. She missed her and worried about her. He wished he had taken her to Hungary after all. Wished he'd given her that small peace of mind.

His desk phone rang. He ignored it, but it

was a reminder that he couldn't stand around brooding all day. He had a business to run, one he'd grown from a nest egg of sweat into a behemoth of technologies that touched millions of lives. Benny's actions could have cost him all of this.

Instead, it would cost all that Gisella's grandmother had built from the sale of that one earring. It would cost them all the sweat and equity she and her children had put into Barsi on Fifth. It would cost Gisella her own career, in the short term, at least. She would never lose the skills she possessed, but without her family's stellar reputation and the prime location in Manhattan, she faced an uphill battle reestablishing herself.

She would recover and make it, he knew she would. She had her grandmother's feisty spirit that way. But she shouldn't *have* to.

God, she'd been cute that day when he'd shown her the earring. Like a little girl giving a presentation at school, teaching him the vocabulary of her trade, so enraptured by her topic she'd been sparkling brighter than the dazzling arrangement of diamonds and blue sapphires set in polished yellow gold.

She was a very accomplished sketch artist, too, whisking a pen across the page as she drew sections of the earring and made notations.

He had watched her and felt something he couldn't name. Affection and admiration, but something deeper, too. Like he wanted to somehow preserve her. Not for himself, although he had wanted that, too, but for the world. She had seemed precious and important to humanity. A gift that was somehow in his life through no good deed of his own.

Then she had handed back the earring, not wanting it. Not wanting him to think she was sleeping with him for it. When they had made love that last time, it had been like nothing he'd ever known. Like she had broken open his chest and gathered his soul against hers. It should have hurt, but it had been relief from a pain he'd lived with so long, he'd forgotten it was a part of him.

It was back now. It multiplied daily, like

an infection eating away at him. Every time he thought back to that last conversation, he agonized.

You are worth loving.

He had been so sure she was trying to take advantage of him, yet here he was *willing* her to come to him. He *wanted* her to ask him for help. He rubbed the back of his neck. Swore. Went and looked at the damned earring *again*.

Was it cursed? Because it seemed to bring heartache, not joy. He rubbed the middle of his chest where the hollow throb never let up.

His phone rang again and he swore, not giving a damn who was calling or whether his company thrived or failed. How could he care about something so inconsequential when Gisella was hurting? She had to be terrified. Her foundation—her family—was under attack.

He stood there with his hands braced on his desk, head hanging, eyes closed, and finally he understood. He understood why her grandmother was standing by her grandson despite the fact his actions could cost her everything she had worked her entire life to build. He understood why Eszti had sold the earring, despite its being a cherished gift from the father of her unborn child. What did objects matter when people you cared about needed looking after?

He lifted his head and cataloged the things he had been so anxious to preserve and protect. The cut crystal glasses and forty-year-old Scotch that stood over a wine fridge full of limited-edition bubbly. The hand-loomed rug, the shelving of two-hundred-year-old reclaimed cedar, the tricked-out entertainment center and the modern art. The prime location overlooking the bay.

What did owning any of this matter if Gisella was hurting and he didn't use every last stick of it to alleviate her pain?

I love you, Kaine.

Could he trust that declaration? He didn't know, but his heart hammered while the rest of him clenched in the anguish of realizing for absolute certain that *he* was in love with *her*.

* * *

Gisella was going crazy. With Barsi on Fifth being dragged into Benny's investigation, she'd been barred from working—which was her outlet for stress. It was also her income and right now the shop was closed, all assets frozen. Her father's company had taken a huge hit, which had stopped her allowance, too.

Despite that, she and her mother had offered to sell the house to help with Benny's legal fees, or at least mortgage it. That meant meetings and assessors tramping through. She and her mother were starting to look for something smaller, talking about how many possessions they would have to divest, which also had her brain headed toward meltdown.

Now her stress level was being ratcheted higher with a video call from Rozi, their first proper talk since before Rozi had left for Hungary.

Gisella was holed up in her room, blankets gathered around her, trying to pretend all her visible angst was for Benny when she was secretly nursing the worst broken heart in history—not that she could complain about it since absolutely no one wanted to hear that she was in love with Kaine Michaels.

"If the charges were cleared up a week ago, why are you still in Hungary?" she asked Rozi.

"I want to come home, I do, but... Don't tell Mom, okay? But... I'm pregnant."

"What?"

"I know, I know. Viktor said he wanted to marry me, but that was before. We can't make announcements, not without it impacting his family and business. How bad is it there?"

"Bad," Gisella said hopelessly.

"I can't ask Viktor—" Her reluctance was obvious.

"We're figuring things out." She wouldn't even consider going to Kaine. "We'll get through this. It'll be messy and maybe we'll all move into your parents' house, but it'll bring us closer, right?"

Rozi looked like she was going to burst into tears. "I miss everyone *so much*. And I feel horrible, Gizi. Morning sick and so guilty I'm not there. I want to curl up and cry."

"Do you want me to come?"

"You can't, can you? I mean, the cost…?"

"And it might look suspicious, like I'm fleeing the country or something. We're being watched. They're probably monitoring this conversation right now. It's a total nightmare, Rozi. You're smart to stay out of it as long as you can."

"I still feel horrible about it. And keeping this baby from Mom? She would want to come, but there's no way they can afford it, not now. There's nothing you or anyone can do here, anyway."

"I could hold your hair," Gisella suggested.

"Yeah, Viktor has about had it with that, I think." She sighed, looking off to the right, but with a profile more hopeless than anything.

"Is he there?"

"No. He's at work."

"Rozi… Is it just morning sickness? Because you look…" Gisella searched her cousin's pale face. "Do you love him?"

Rozi closed her eyes. "This just happened. I didn't mean to get pregnant. I know we promised each other—"

"Oh, my God, Rozi. I'm not *judging*. I was sleeping with Kaine. I know exactly how it happens. That was a silly promise we made as kids. No, I'm saying, if you're not in love… This isn't Grandmamma's time. You can come home and we'll take care of you."

"How?" Rozi asked with an edge of hysteria. "Barsi on Fifth is going down the toilet." She sniffed and drew a calming breath. "Viktor and I are working things out. He said he would set me up with a workshop when I'm ready. For the sake of the baby—and Grandmamma—I have to give marriage a try. I mean, she married Grandpapa out of necessity, right? It can work."

Gisella could tell Rozi was saying it to convince herself more than her.

"There's actually more we need to talk about with the earrings."

"I know, but I think I'm going to be sick again," Rozi said in a pained voice. "I have to go. I'm sorry to dump all this on you and ask you to keep it secret. I had to talk it out. But it's better if everyone just thinks I'm stuck in limbo here."

"If you're sure. I love you. I miss you."

"Me, too." She swore and apologized again before she abruptly ended the call.

Gisella sniffed, feeling teary, but envious. She was definitely not pregnant. She'd found that out a couple days after leaving Kaine's penthouse. But falling in love and having children alongside Rozi was a fantasy she hadn't consciously acknowledged until it was denied her. Their life events had always been in such lockstep. It left her quite bereft that Rozi was moving on to a new one without her.

Her melancholy was overshadowed by her concern for Rozi, though. What must she be feeling, contemplating marriage to a man she barely knew while navigating the physical and emotional toll of an unplanned pregnancy?

To hell with it. She would go to Budapest and she didn't care who said she couldn't!

Of course, her bank balance had an opinion, but she'd figure something out. She dragged her laptop back onto her thighs, thinking to look up how much cash she could scrape together when she saw the flash of her ring—the one Rozi had made for her.

Huh.

She set aside her laptop and dressed for a visit to the pawnshop.

CHAPTER ELEVEN

GISELLA WAS FEELING so defiant, she caught a cab at the end of the block, eschewing the much cheaper subway for a direct trip to a reputable broker she knew personally. She called him from the cab to ensure he could see her.

Along with her uncle, she and Rozi often scoped the wares in pawnshops, picking up gems and scrap gold. Jerry, the owner of this particular establishment, was a diamond in the rough. He always wore a shirt that didn't fit and a lingering odor of cigar smoke, but he was sharp and fair and had a good eye. They concluded their business in a matter of seconds and were ending on a handshake when another customer walked in.

Or rather—

"Kaine?" Her heart took flight so high and fast, she grew light-headed.

"What are you doing here?" he demanded.

"I asked you first."

"I was coming to see you when I saw you get into a cab." He looked at her ring still sitting on a small mat of black velvet Jerry had set on his glass counter, as was his habit for examining a piece. "What are you doing? You're not selling that." His voice tightened with accusation.

"I need some money to go see Rozi—"

"She's still in Hungary?" He took out his wallet and set his limitless credit card onto the counter with a snap. "Whatever you want for it."

"You can't buy it." She showed him the ticket she had stuffed into her pocket. "I have a month to buy it back myself before— Hey!"

Kaine plucked the slip out of her fingers and handed it to Jerry, jerking his head at the credit card. "Make it happen." Then he picked up her ring and grabbed her hand, trying to put it on the wrong finger.

"This one," she mumbled, relaxing when it was back where it belonged. She had steeled herself to say goodbye to it and was deeply glad she didn't have to, but, "Now I just have to give you this." She pulled her wad of cash from her purse, short the 15 percent Jerry shamelessly made as he rang the charge onto Kaine's credit card.

Kaine ignored the cash, pocketed his card and held the door for her. "My car is—there." He took her arm and they quickly ducked into the backseat. "Why the hell would you do that?" He looked genuinely angry. "Is Rozi okay? Why isn't she home yet?"

She sighed toward the roof of the car, head tilted against the seat back. "That's a bit of a story. She's okay, yes. Not in jail. That's been cleared up. But she has to stay and…" She swallowed. "I miss her."

"And you're so short on cash, you were going to sell the ring she made you."

"Quit yelling at me! I didn't *want* to. But it's one of the few things that isn't tied up with Benny's investigation."

"You could have come to me. Asked me for help."

"You know my feelings on that and I know yours. Here." She waved the cash at him again, silently demanding he take it.

He glared at her as he plucked it from her grip and stuffed it back into her open purse. Then he shoved the bag firmly into her lap.

"Why are you here?" she grumbled, zipping the purse so the money wouldn't fly out when she wasn't paying attention.

"I want to see your mother. Is she home?"

"Mom? No. She's one of the few of us who still has a job. Why do you need to see her? Some app emergency that can only be solved by a lesson in feminist history?"

"That sarcasm," he said, running his hand down his face.

"What about it?"

"I *miss* it."

She stared, astonished, but they arrived at her house and he got out to hold the door for her.

"Coffee?" she asked as she let him in and walked straight through to the kitchen.

"Did you dismiss your housekeeper?" he asked as he followed.

"Day off. Mom told her she might want to look for something, though, just in case. Grandmamma might move in here with us and sell her apartment. We haven't figured everything out, yet."

"It's bad, though."

"It is, yes." She sighed. "A lot of the Barsi assets have been frozen. We have no idea for how long."

"I wish you had called me, Gisella."

She finished grinding the beans before saying heavily, "You know why I couldn't, Kaine." She tamped the grounds into the filter on the espresso maker she had bought for her mother a few Christmases ago. "I can't ask you for anything or you'll think I'm prevailing on our...relationship."

Silence.

She wrenched the filter into place and set

the tiny cups, then hit the start button. Ignored the angry fire behind her breastbone.

"Not that we have one. A relationship, I mean."

"Of course we do. And you *need* my help. Admit that much, at least."

She looked to the ceiling for deliverance.

"When your mother gets back, I'm going to ask her how much you need to stay afloat through all of this. I'd go to Benny or his father, but I suspect they'd let pride get in the way. Your mother is more practical. If she refuses, I'm going to your grandmother."

Heat, the airless kind in a dry sauna, seemed to suck the oxygen from her lungs. "You don't owe me anything, Kaine."

"It's not a transaction. It's not even a gift. It's..." He sent an agitated hand through his hair. "That morning in San Francisco, when I cornered you into posing as my lover, you said you were cooperating with my demands to absorb or deflect the pain that might otherwise hit the rest of your family. That you knew it would cost you and you wanted to do it anyway. I want to be that kind of buffer for you."

She reached blindly for the edge of the countertop, knees wobbling along with her heart seesawing in her chest.

"But…" Did he remember everything she'd said that morning? *Why* she had been willing to do that?

He did. She could see it in the way his fist went white with tension. She didn't even think he was breathing. He just stared into her like he was willing something from her, but his jaw was locked up tight.

She took a faltering step toward him. "Does that mean—" She couldn't finish, could only look from one of his eyes to the other.

"Did I kill it in you, Gisella? I've been so scared that making you leave with Benny that night destroyed anything you might have felt for me."

She swallowed, fearful of relinquishing all her defenses again and being rejected, but she also knew she had to be honest. More open and honest than she'd ever been in her life.

"My love isn't that fragile, Kaine." Her eyes grew hot, her throat tight. "I'm hurt and angry, but I still love you." Her limbs felt disjointed as she took a few steps toward him. "I tried to prove it to you—"

"I'm trying to prove mine for *you*. That's why I'm here."

She faltered, swelling with so much emotion she was a bubble, thin-skinned and ready to burst. "You love me?"

"So much I don't have words."

"Words are fine. Words are all I need. I don't need a gesture. I don't want your money. It's enough that you're here." She moved close enough to set her hand on his chest, felt the way his heart pounded in time to the tattoo of her pulse in her throat.

"Don't reject my offer, Gisella." He slid his hand down the side of her head, trapping her hair against her neck. "Family helps family, right? If I want to become part of this family…"

She realized he was holding something out to her with his other hand. A faded velvet box.

"In lieu of an engagement ring. Although, I gave you a really nice ring a little while ago, one I know you already love—"

"Kaine." Her mouth wobbled. She was unable to decide if she wanted to smile or break down into emotive tears. She touched her lips with trembling fingers, trying to steady herself.

"Will you? Marry me?"

"You." She grasped the open edge of his jacket. "I'll marry *you*. Not your fortune."

"It's kind of a package deal."

"If I have to, then. *Fine.*" She threw herself against him and he dragged her in tight.

He shuddered as she twined her arms around his waist and crammed her wet face into his shoulder.

"I missed you, too," she said on a sniff.

"Yeah. This feels really good. I love you, Gisella. I love you more than I know how to express." His hand fisted in her hair as he kissed her temple and her cheekbone and searched for the corner of her mouth.

They kissed, sweet and hot. It grew anguished and desperate. They drew back.

"We have time," she said.

He nodded. "We do. A lifetime."

They smiled, then kissed again. Slower. Deeper.

With all the love they had in them.

Two weeks later, progress had been made on Benny's case. The investigation was ongoing, but it looked very much like Benny would avoid jail time. The doors at Barsi on Fifth were allowed to open again, too.

Gisella was back at work, but only to finish the projects she'd already started. She hadn't accepted any new commissions because today was her last day. She was moving to San Francisco with Kaine after her engagement party tonight.

Her mother thought she was rushing things, but had agreed to host the party. All the family was coming, including Gisella's father and his wife. Grandmamma was thrilled with the engagement. She heartily approved of Kaine. Everyone was eager to meet him.

Even Rozi turned up pale and sheepish, but beaming. She opened her arms and Gisella rushed her, hugging her with all she had in her while the rest of the family went crazy around them.

When she finally pulled away, she introduced Kaine, but everyone wanted to know what had happened to Rozi in Hungary.

"Let Kaine and Gisella have their moment!" Rozi insisted. "You can hear all my news later."

Gisella was dying to get her alone and hear everything firsthand herself, but before she knew it, another surprise guest had arrived.

Rozi bit her lip as Viktor Rohan entered, looking for his fiancée. He moved directly to Rozi's side and stayed glued to her hip. He was tall and reserved, very smooth and urbane as he met everyone, but impossible to read. At the same time, there was something familiar that went beyond the photo Gisella had seen of him. It was weirdly endearing.

They left early. Rozi wasn't feeling well, but Viktor invited Gisella and Kaine to join them for brunch in the morning.

"What did you think of him?" she asked Kaine later that night, when they were snuggled in her childhood bedroom, replete from lovemaking.

"He's a lot like you and your mom."

"What?" She came up on an elbow. "I thought he was acting like an elite-force bodyguard, the way he was shadowing Rozi so closely."

"So were you," he pointed out drily.

"Hmmph. Well, if you hadn't tied him up asking if he still wanted Grandmamma's earring, I wouldn't have had a minute alone with her. Did you come to terms, by the way?"

"We did. How did it go with Rozi?"

She loved how genuinely concerned he sounded.

"I was hoping she was happy. Like us." She snuggled into his side. "If I'm still worried after brunch tomorrow, I'm going to tell her she can come live with us in San Francisco."

"All right."

"I was joking. She's planning to go back to Hungary."

"It's going to be hard for you to be that far from her."

"It will be hard to be away from everyone. But I have you." She slid against him.

"You humble me, Gisella." He stopped playing with her hair and kissed her. "I'm terrified I won't be able to live up to your expectations, but I want to try."

"You already do."

EPILOGUE

One year later...

GISELLA STIFLED A yawn and said good-night to Christina, her store manager. "I'll lock up."

She flicked the bolt, turned off the "Open" sign of Barsi on the Bay and came back to where her husband was pouring fresh glasses of champagne. He set them on the case where her grandmother's earrings were displayed with a sign that read, "On loan from the Rohan family." The earrings' history was a popular hit on their website and had drawn half the crowd that had come for opening day.

"Nice work, beautiful."

"Thank you. I'm pretty impressed myself." She clinked and let a few bubbles touch her tongue, then yawned again.

"You've been working too hard," he scolded.

"The store is open now. Ease up. Christina seems to have a firm hand on everything. No micromanaging."

"Says the workaholic, but I plan to. She is a good fit, isn't she?"

"It's the Martìnez genes. You can't expect anything less than excellence."

"Hmm, no. Of course not." Shortly after they got engaged, Gisella had gently pushed him toward checking in with his mother's family one more time. His cousin Christina had been working in Sacramento. They'd met up several times, all getting along like a house on fire.

Christina was Gisella's age, funny and bright and earnest. She'd had a form of childhood leukemia, which had been the reason her parents hadn't been allowed to take in Kaine, despite wanting to. They had tried to reach out later, but he had been in juvenile detention by then and they weren't allowed to contact him. Christina had been the one to find him online and reach out for her *quinceañera* after reading about him.

Her parents were kind people, older and didn't travel much. She had a younger brother who was at school, but planned to stay with Christina this summer and spend some time getting to know *tío* Kaine.

When Gisella had been hiring for the store, Christina had jokingly put her name in the hat. Her management background had been a good fit and Kaine had warned, "If you don't hire her, I will."

Gisella liked having someone so trustworthy in that position, especially when her attention was about to be split in a whole new direction.

"Problem?" Kaine asked, nodding at the champagne she abruptly set aside. "It tastes fine to me. Neither of us is driving."

"No, but…" She linked her hands before her. "You remember when we were visiting in New York and Rozi brought the baby and Grandmamma said she hoped it was contagious when I was holding him?"

"Yes."

She let him connect the dots.

His confused frown fell into stunned lines. He dropped his flute. It shattered and splashed champagne all over their shoes, making both of them jolt.

"How can you be shocked?" Gisella asked. "We agreed we both wanted this. I went off birth control that night."

"It was three weeks ago. It doesn't happen that fast! Does it?"

She shrugged. "It did for Rozi."

He looked so astonished, she didn't know how to take it.

"Are you okay with this news?" she asked tentatively.

"I honestly didn't think I could be happier." He still sounded astounded. "You give me so much, Gisella. I don't know how..."

"You helped me make this store happen! You helped Benny and the rest of my family. Every day, you give me *you*. Now you're giving me a baby. One that will make Grandmamma so happy. *I'm* already so happy..." She was going to cry.

He cupped her face and kissed her.

She stepped closer, shoes crunching on the broken glass.

He stooped and picked her up, set her on the glass case. Gave her a rueful look. "I had plans to christen this store in another way, not throw glass and champagne all over the place. But if you're pregnant, I think a bed would be the more gentlemanly choice."

"There's a sofa in my office."

He narrowed his eyes, then nodded approvingly. "I love your problem-solving abilities. Always have."

Later, after making love and dressing, sweeping up the glass and mopping the floor, they had his driver take them to the beach, where they held hands and watched the sun set on another glorious day in the life they were building together.

* * * * *